BIG, BAD GRUFF

Big City Lycans
Book Two

New York Times and USA Today Bestselling Author

Eve Langlais

Copyright Big, Bad, Gruff © Eve Langlais

Cover Art © by Melony Paradise of ParadiseCoverDesign.com

Produced in Canada

Published by Eve Langlais

http://www.EveLanglais.com

eBook: ISBN: 978 1 77 384 3568

Print ISBN: 978 1 77 384 3575

ALL RIGHTS RESERVED

This book is a work of fiction and the characters, events and dialogue found within the story are of the author's imagination and are not to be construed as real. Any resemblance to actual events or persons, either living or deceased, is completely coincidental.

No part of this book may be reproduced or shared in any form or by any means, electronic or mechanical, including but not limited to digital copying, file sharing, audio recording, email and printing without permission in writing from the author.

PROLOGUE

Years ago, when Billy was just a kid...

"Bitch, I'll give you something to whine about!"

"Fuck you," was the screamed reply.

Billy lay in his bed, listening as his parents fought. Again. He should have been used to it by now. After all, they'd been doing it as far back as he could remember, usually over stupid stuff.

For example, tonight Mom made meatloaf, which nobody liked, yet they got it at least once a week because when the ground beef went on sale, it was cheap as fuck to make—or so Mom claimed. To render it edible required a lot of ketchup, a shit-ton according to his dad, only when Billy's dad went to squirt some on the dry-looking hunk, all he got was that farting noise and a little squirt of the red stuff.

Slamming it down, Dad snapped, "Get me a new bottle."

Which led to Mom saying, "I ain't got one. Ain't doing groceries until next week."

No ketchup? Billy eyed his portion of meat and inwardly cringed. Salt could only do so much.

"I can't fucking eat this." Dad shoved at the plate, a discontented set to his jaw.

"Don't be such a fucking baby. I got some ketchup packets in the car. Billy, go grab them."

Billy fled quickly to the rusted vehicle parked outside their mobile home. Duct tape held the rear passenger door closed. Strapping wound around the bumper to hold it in place. Mom had been told last time she got pulled over by the cops to junk it, but as she claimed, "It's mine and I'll drive it if I want to." She ignored the tickets stuffed in her glove box.

Billy scrounged through the car, checking the glovebox, the console, even the floor, to find some ketchup packets. He found three vinegars, a ton of salt, some pepper, and two ketchup sachets of dubious age.

He brought them back in and dropped them onto the table. Dad snatched them and squirted them on the hunk of now-cold meat. Barely enough red stuff for two bites.

Dad eyed it with a grimace. "This is bullshit. How am I supposed to eat this garbage?"

Billy would have preferred not to as well, but that would just cause more trouble. Instead, he faked it, pretending to eat while dropping hunks on the floor for their fat pit bull, Buddy, who gobbled them up. What did it say that only the dog liked it?

"It's not that bad." Mom shoveled hers in and chewed open-mouthed to prove a point.

It didn't go over well. Dad, hungry after working all day, was pissed. "Don't you get an attitude with me, you lazy fucking cow. I go to work all day and get to come home to this crap." The plate went flying off the table with a crash.

Mom shoved away from the table. "You asshole. You think I got time to make you gourmet fucking meals? I work too."

"As a cashier." Dad sneered.

"Which is harder than slugging garbage into a truck."

"At least I bring home a good paycheck," Dad countered, getting to his feet and glaring at Mom.

She snorted. "Which you drink away or gamble in those poker games. I'm the one paying most of the bills and making all the meals."

"Because that's a woman's job."

That would be the point Billy began oozing out of his chair carefully, quietly, lest they notice and drag him into the upcoming rumble.

His parents stood nose to nose.

"You're a sexist pig!" Mom retorted.

"Says the woman who rarely vacuums."

"Would it kill you fucking run it once in a while? I do everything around here."

And so it went...

Billy hid in his room, a thing he did a lot, while his parents battled. It was hours of on-and-off screaming. Crashing. And then the most annoying part, the sex as they made up. Loud and boisterous, there was no way to muffle the noise.

No way to escape the hellhole of his family life. His parents, for all that they hated each other, just wouldn't get divorced.

And the cycle of violence went on until the day they decided to fight while driving on the highway with Billy in the back. The fact he wore his seatbelt saved his life.

Alas, his parents didn't walk away from that crash.

It could have been a terrible thing to happen to a teenager suddenly thrust into the foster care system. It turned out to be a blessing. With his foster family, Billy finally got three square meals a day—delicious meals—plus snacks. No more meatloaf. No more yelling or fighting. He even made friends with the boys living on the massive ranch nearby.

After graduating, he went on to become a cop, detective to be exact, which turned out to be a huge asset to his pack when Billy got bitten and became a werewolf.

1

"It's so unfair," Brandy muttered as yet one more internet search on how to become a werewolf let her down. Why was it only boys could become hairy on the full moon? Like seriously, anyone who'd seen Brandy's legs and pits during shark week would have totally pegged her for being some kind of hairy shapeshifter. But no, she was just plain ol' Brandy Herman, a nurse in her thirties, whose only exciting claims to fame were that she could belch the alphabet and make a mean meatloaf.

"How many more appointments left for the day?" Maeve asked, leaning against her desk. She gave a slight cough into her hand. Not the first one that day. Brandy's best friend had begun looking unwell mid-afternoon.

Brandy's lips pursed. "None because you're going home."

"I can't. Mrs. Johnson is due for a refill."

Brandy slid the requisition sheet to her. "Which I already printed, so just sign here." She pointed. "Now, no more excuses. Get your ass to bed. We can't have you sick for your own wedding." Which was in less than a week and Brandy still didn't have a date. Good thing there'd be a few single guys attending the reception. If only she hadn't already placed most of them in the friend zone.

"I don't know what's wrong. It hit me so suddenly." Maeve slumped.

"Probably some new corona mutation. I'll reschedule tomorrow. That, along with the weekend, should give you time to recover."

Maeve hesitated. "I don't want to leave you alone." Their receptionist, Marco, had gone on a vacation with his husband.

"I'll be out of here before dinnertime. Just a few things to take care of. I'll be fine."

Maeve chewed her lower lip. "Are you sure?"

"Git before I call Griffin."

"Don't do that. He'll try and carry me home."

Brandy grinned. "Try? We both know the moment he finds out you're sick he's going to coddle the heck out of you."

"He will." Maeve reached for her coat with a smile.

About time she'd found herself a guy who melted her inside and out. Now, if only Brandy could have the same luck. Unfortunately for her, the guy who melted her panties had been staying far, far away.

"Text me when you get home," Brandy demanded.

Maeve lived only a few blocks away, but since they'd both been kidnapped a few months ago by some douchebags who wanted some family heirloom, they'd gotten a little more safety conscious. Avoiding being abducted by psychos in the future seemed a good idea.

"I will text you and see if Ulric can head over so you're not alone."

"Don't be silly. I'll be fine. He'll just mess up my desk again with those massive feet." For a time after meeting him, Brandy had thought about dating Ulric. He provided security for Maeve's fiancé, Griffin, aka head honcho alpha of the pack and owner of a pot shop.

I have the coolest friends.

Platonic friends at that. Ulric was good looking, a werewolf, and nice, too. Only problem? She saw him more as a brother than a lover.

"Lock the door."

"I will, and you text me the moment you walk in the door."

"Yes, Mom," Maeve promised with a roll of her eyes before she left.

Brandy flicked the thumb-lock and made quick work of rescheduling. Only one person complained. She mentioned the phrase "possible coronavirus infection" and suddenly Mr. Lambskin didn't need his appointment so urgently anymore. It wasn't as if he were actually sick. He just liked to come in at least once a month and demand Maeve run tests because he'd convinced himself he had a new ailment. Someone needed to take his internet away.

A package arrived that required a signature for the receipt. She juggled the box into the storage room. On the way back to her desk, her phone went off.

A few emails popped in, mostly junk trying to convince their new medical office to try some products. A few inquiries as to how to become a patient and one that had definite creep vibes, given all it said was, *I'll see you soon*. Instant block and delete. This made about a dozen now she'd received in the last month, ranging from *I'm watching* to *We belong together*.

Discomfiting, and yet she'd not told Maeve. Her best friend had enough to deal with. After all, she was engaged to a werewolf.

So lucky.

As Brandy grabbed her purse and jacket, getting ready to leave, the door opened. Had she locked it after the package? Obviously not.

She whirled. "We're closed—" A shove sent her stumbling into the reception desk then flailing as she fought off the hands grabbing at her.

"Let go!" she screeched, managing to wrench free. She whirled to see her attacker.

A face, drawn and hollow, the eyes bright with

addiction, stared at her. The mouth was putrid as he asked through rotted teeth, "Where is it?"

Having worked the emergency room for years, Brandy knew what he wanted. "We don't keep drugs here."

"Liar. This is a doctor's office. Where is it? I need something." He lunged at her.

Brandy considered herself somewhat fit, and she'd taken defense classes. Those didn't help much against someone desperate for a fix, exhibiting super strength and a lack of empathy. She slapped at his hands while ducking and weaving, caught against the desk. She had to avoid him getting a grip.

He moved fast and managed to grab her neck with one hand. Before she could yank free, he had the second one squeezing. She grabbed at him, gasping, eyes wide.

I'm going to die.

He shoved her backwards, bending her over the desk, pressing against her.

Panic hit her as she clawed at his grip.

His spittle flew as he rasped out, "Give it. Give it."

She couldn't even reply, but even if she could have, she had nothing to give.

He slammed her head off the desk.

She saw spots. *Wham.*

"Give. Me!"

He wanted it? Then let him have it. Her knee finally got its knobby end together and rose to strike.

The blow would have put most men on the floor, but the addict simply offered a putrid gasp. She almost puked and rolled to avoid it, which was when she saw the stapler by the printouts she'd been filing.

She grabbed it and swung. Missed, but the way the addict swayed allowed her to slip away and gain some separation, enough that she could find a weapon. The only thing she could actually grab and swing? Her computer monitor.

He staggered and shook his head. The guy was too strung out to realize he might be in trouble. "Bitch. Give me the shit."

"I said there's nothing here." She compounded her statement with another swing of the monitor, losing her grip on the impact as it collided. It proved to be enough.

The violent junkie dropped in a heap, and she stood over him, glaring. "No means no."

It was only as she saw the glint of a knife in his pocket that it hit her. She'd been lucky. He could have chosen to slash and stab instead of trying to cave in her skull.

Her fingers went to her throbbing temple, and she swallowed through a tender throat. She set the broken monitor back on the desk then grabbed her phone. She dialed nine then hesitated, finger poised over the one.

Calling the emergency line would bring cops and questioning, probably a few hours of it, as well as paperwork, when she could be curling up on her couch with her new kitten, sucking back leftover Chinese food while watching *Warrior Nun* on Netflix. Not to mention, it would be a lot of hassle for nothing. The police tended to do catch-and-release on what they considered petty crime. The fact she'd fought off the assault worked against her. The more she debated, the less she wanted to deal with law enforcement. The problem being she couldn't exactly leave the unconscious wannabe robber on the office floor, nor just toss him into the street.

If she called Maeve, she'd rush back, sick or not. Actually, just about everyone she knew that wouldn't blink at moving a body would most likely tell Maeve. Snitches.

It left her only one option. If he answered his phone. Which he didn't. So Brandy fired off a text. *Attacked in office. Need help.*

Within seconds, there was a reply. *On my way.*

Just in case the druggie woke up before the cavalry arrived, she snared some medical tape and took care of his wrists then the ankles for good measure.

Then she sat down and waited for the sexy and oh-so-standoffish Detective Billy Gruff. And yes, she'd had a good internal giggle at his expense the first time she heard his name. Who did that to their kid?

That mockery never slipped past her lips, mostly because she was too busy flirting with the sexy man in the ill-fitting suit jacket. They'd first met because Griffin Lanark, Maeve's fiancé, ended up in the emergency room with bullet holes. They weren't engaged at the time, of course. A love story of a patient and his doctor.

When a handsome detective came around asking questions, Brandy had batted her lashes and made her interest clear.

Detective Gruff ignored all of her flirting and acted completely uninterested, even as he'd given her his cell number written on the back of a card in case she ever needed to contact him. A few nights she was almost tempted to try sexting him to see if he'd play along.

Instead, she ended up asking him for help when some thugs kidnapped Maeve and her, after some family cookbook that was worth a fortune. He came to the rescue, along with some friends, which was how she discovered that sexy Billy Gruff wasn't a goat but a Lycan. As in a furry, four-legged werewolf. It only made him sexier. Pity it wasn't mutual.

Brandy had known the guy for a few months, not that she saw him often because even she drew the line at committing a crime to end up in an interrogation room for alone-time. But now she had a legitimate reason to put out a cry for help. While keeping an eye on the body on the floor, she dug in her purse, freshening her gloss, brushing her hair. She also popped a piece of gum into her mouth. After all, didn't werewolves have a super sense of smell?

Quicker than expected, a knock sounded at the door, which her dumb ass had forgotten to lock. Again.

Good thing no one walked in. The guy that she'd taken the precaution of tying up with medical tape might have been hard to explain.

Brandy headed for the door and opened it to see a harried detective. He eyed her up and down. "Are you okay?"

She almost said, "I am now that you're here," but she wanted his help, not to send him fleeing.

"I'm fine. Get inside, quick." Once he entered, she locked the door. No more surprises.

The detective glared down at the trussed tweaker. "Not sure why you texted." He waved a hand. "Looks like you've already got things handled."

"I need help getting rid of him."

"Call 911."

"Oh please, hours of paperwork for him to be released in the morning? You're part of the wolf mob in Ottawa. Shouldn't you do something about him?"

His lips pinched. "He's an addict. He needs rehab."

"He's a criminal with no moral compass who tried to choke me and bash in my skull for drugs, even after I told him we had none." Brandy huffed, peeved at his blatant dismissal of the danger.

The detective finally glanced at her, his gaze lingering on her throat, which throbbed almost as badly as her head. By tomorrow, she'd have some lovely bruises.

Billy's jaw tensed. "I thought you said you were okay."

"I am. Mostly. Nothing a few Tylenols won't fix."

"He hurt you." A grim statement.

She shrugged. "Yeah, but in good news, I'm not bleeding or dying."

A low sound emerged from the man, and Billy turned from her to eye the body on the floor. "I'll handle this. Go home."

"What—"

"Go. Home."

"But I can help you."

His gaze narrowed on her. "Now, Brandy." Despite his obvious annoyance, she wanted to brush the lock of dark hair that had flopped onto his forehead. Probably not the right time. He might just bite off her hand.

"Was just offering some help. No need to be snappy," she grumbled, putting on her coat and grabbing her purse.

"Where's your car?" he asked.

"I don't currently have one." Stupid motor blew up on her last one, and she'd been hemming on getting a replacement since she could now walk to work.

He frowned. "How are you getting home?"

"My two feet. It's what keeps my ass so tight." She tossed him a sassy wink, and his nostrils flared.

"I'll drive you."

"No need." She tossed her head. "It's not far."

"Get in my car, Brandy."

"What about..." She gestured to the druggie.

"I'm giving you a ride, and that's final. I'm parked out front." He handed her a set of keys. "Pop the trunk once you get in."

"Are you seriously going to toss him into your trunk?"

"How else am I getting rid of him?"

"We can't bring him out the front. It's barely dark. People will notice. I'll drive your car around back. Meet me at the exit in the rear."

His lips flattened. "We'll both go."

She put a hand on his arm. "Don't be silly. I'll be out of sight like thirty seconds."

"Hmmph." His grunted reply. He walked her to the door and then stood in the doorway, watching as she got behind the wheel. By the time she'd gone to the edge of the building and crawled down the alley to the loading door at the back, he was there waiting.

He leaned down, and she cycled the window a crack. "Hey, good-looking, need a ride?" she teased.

With not even a hint of a smile, he grumbled, "Pop the trunk."

It took a second to locate the button. She pressed it and then got out of the car, doing her best to eyeball any cameras in the alley. Just the one above their door, which she knew Griffin's tech guy had access to.

Billy emerged with a bulging fabric bag, which he lugged into the trunk. Then another, which made her frown. He then clearly asked, "Is that all the laundry?"

She caught on quick. "Yeah, thanks for giving me a hand. Stupid me forgot to schedule a pickup."

He closed the door to the clinic, ensuring it latched and locked before getting into the driver's seat. She'd already slid over to the passenger side. Truth be told, she wasn't feeling too hot. Her head and throat throbbed as the adrenaline of panic wore off and a chill hit her.

"You cold?" he asked as if he could sense her shiver.

Before she could reply, he'd turned on the heated seat and cranked the blower inside the car.

He pulled out of the alley and turned right without asking. Forget telling him where she lived. Apparently, the detective already knew. Stalking her or more likely as part of his duties in providing security for Griffin and the pack.

"You're being too quiet," he remarked. "Is your throat tight? Can you breathe?"

"I'm fine." Barely raspy. And to prove she was coherent, she added, "Feel free to give me mouth-to-mouth if you're worried."

The sudden screech of brakes jolted Brandy as he stopped in front of the converted house where she'd scored the second floor as her new digs.

He drummed his fingers on the steering wheel. "Lock the door when you get inside."

"Yes, sir." Offered with a sassy salute. "Thanks for coming to the rescue."

"Next time call the cops." His terse reply.

That caused a cheeky dimpled smile. "I did. I called you."

He gave her a stare.

"Thanks again, Detective Gruff."

"Call me Billy." He appeared to regret it just as quickly as he said it, given he scowled.

"Thanks, Billy." She pushed on the passenger door to open it, and before she could step out, Billy stood there, offering her a hand. Holy fast. He hauled her to her feet and didn't let go right away.

She glanced up at him. "Thank you again. I don't know the last time a gentleman helped me out of a car." Those kinds of old-school manners had been disappearing in the last decade. Great, given it showed women being treated more equally. Boo, because there was something to be said about those tiny gestures.

"Second floor, right?" he asked, glancing at the stairs.

"Yup." She headed for the steps and wasn't entirely surprised he followed close behind.

The small balcony outside her door barely had room for the two of them. She pulled her keys from her handbag, but her hand shook. Not because of the attack. Having Billy close did strange things to her. He unlocked the door and cracked it open before handing back her keys.

"Are you sure you're all right?" he asked. "Maybe we should call Maeve and have her check you out."

She snorted. "You do realize I'm capable of diagnosing myself. I don't have a concussion."

"You can't be sure," he replied.

"No nausea. No double vision. No confusion. Or any other symptoms other than an achy head."

"Do you want me to stick around?" he offered.

She really, really wanted to say yes... "Probably not a good idea given what's in your trunk."

Billy glanced down, and his lips flattened. "Guess I'll be going then."

As he took the first step away, she blurted out, "Hey, I don't suppose you want to be my plus-one for the wedding?"

His brows shot up. "What?"

"You know, Maeve and Griffin's wedding. I'm allowed to bring a guest."

"And? It's not like I wasn't invited. Given my job, I'm not supposed to associate with them." A detective shouldn't hang with a pot store owner, never mind the fact Griffin ran it legally.

"But see, if you go as my date, it's plausible deniability," she countered.

"It's a bad idea," he replied before he bounded down the rest of the steps and jumped into his car. He practically left rubber on the asphalt he peeled away so fast.

When am I going to accept the fact he's just not interested?

Yet for a guy who supposedly didn't care, he'd

come running twice when she called for help. Then again, he was a cop. Probably the heroic type that would save anyone in need.

As Brandy entered her apartment, she wondered what he'd do with the guy in the trunk. Decided it was probably best she didn't know so she couldn't testify against him if something happened.

Given the shit day she'd had, she found solace in her new kitten and the tub of chocolate brownie chunk ice cream.

So what if Billy didn't find her attractive. Plenty of guys did.

"Screw you, Detective Gruff," she muttered around a mouthful of cold sugary goodness.

She did screw him. That was if dreams counted. Just like she had almost every night since meeting him.

2

Stuck at a red light, a block away from Brandy's place, Billy slapped the steering wheel. Once. Twice. Fuck it, three times for frustration.

Damn Brandy for dragging him into her presence. He'd been doing his best to avoid her since they'd met. Doing his best to not fantasize about the perky nurse with the sweet curves, even as his own dreams betrayed him and left him sticky when he woke.

He'd been determined to not get involved because he didn't do committed relationships and he could tell she was the type who wanted to settle down.

No way. No how. Not Billy Gruff. He figured out of sight, out of mind. Only it didn't appear to be working.

What did it say about him that she called him for help and he dropped everything to go to her rescue?

Only to arrive and find out she had things under control.

He'd been torn with pride and rage that she'd handled the druggie on her own. Brandy wasn't some wilting damsel in distress. She had the courage to stand up for herself. But it infuriated him that she'd had to defend herself.

When he found out the fucker had dared to hurt her... If she'd not been present, Billy might have lost the famous cool composure he was known for. Might have done the unthinkable, given how hard he'd pulsed with a feeling not usually experienced outside of a full moon.

Blame Brandy. Something about her turned him into a mess. When around her, he couldn't think straight. Felt as if his own body betrayed him, given how it reacted to her scent.

And she'd been harmed.

It took everything in him not to drive to the woods and let loose. Instead, he remained within the city, heading for a neighborhood where nobody ever snitched, especially to cops.

He parked in an alley, the kind with rank dumpsters. No homeless in there currently, as its most recent resident, a fellow simply known as Gray Beard, had died. Liver failure from a lifetime of drinking. Billy slid on some gloves before getting out of his car and popping the trunk. The moment it opened, Billy found himself face to face with the druggie, eyes bloodshot, opening his mouth to yell.

Billy grabbed him by the shirt and hauled him out of the trunk, growling, "Go ahead and scream. No one cares."

"Who are you? Da fuck you want, you perv?" the druggie asked as Billy set him on his feet. The addict had already removed the tape from his wrists and ankles.

"I want you to leave good people alone."

"I'm good people," the fucker insisted.

"You choked a dear friend of mine."

"You talking about that sweet piece of ass?" The man licked his lips. "She's feisty. I'll remember that for next time."

"There won't be a next time," Billy warned. So much for just letting the fucker go. Brandy was right. Even if arrested, he'd be out within a day, two at most, harassing people again. Hurting defenseless women.

Hurting Brandy.

Billy ignored the guy to reach for something kept tucked under the driver seat of his car. He put the emergency kit on the hood.

The druggie wavered on his feet, and then, because he'd obviously fried too many brain cells, boasted, "Oh hell yeah there'll be a next time. I know where she works, mother fucker. I'll bring friends, and we'll have ourselves a good time."

Billy pulled a syringe and bottle from the kit.

"What you got there?" The druggie practically drooled.

"Something that will get you higher than you ever imagined." Billy held the items in his gloved hands. They were already clean of prints given they were part of his emergency stash.

"Gimme!" The druggie lunged, and Billy sidestepped.

"In a second. First, you're going to promise to not share."

"As if." The guy snorted, his hands outstretched, fingers grasping. "Give." The addict's eyes had a crazed light as he agreed to anything for his next fix.

Billy handed it over. He didn't watch as the druggie pulled from the vial and, without any preamble, shot himself in the arm. Immediately, the addict's body relaxed. He slumped to the ground, the needle still sticking out of his flesh, a dumb smirk on his face.

Billy closed the trunk and stowed his emergency kit, which would need a replacement of the insulin he'd just handed off.

The druggie complained as he pulled the needle saying, "This stuff is shit. I'm barely feeling a high."

"Then take some more," Billy encouraged.

As he left, the guy was jabbing himself again. Given the full vial, he had a few shots he could still administer, not that it would take that many. Insulin taken by someone who didn't need it was usually fatal.

There were those that would be appalled at his callousness. In his mind, those willing to hurt others to get high didn't get his sympathy. Not when Brandy's safety was at risk.

Thoughts of her led to him picturing her. How her lips always seemed to curve in happiness. How the corners of her eyes crinkled when she smiled. How she smelled. How she'd almost been killed.

Once more, he worried about her having a concussion. Sure, she'd claimed to be fine, the only reason he'd dropped at home instead of a hospital to check on her. Still, she might not be the best judge of her own condition.

The smart thing would have been to call Griffin and have him send someone over to make sure Brandy was okay. Billy instead found himself outside her place, eyeing the windows to her apartment. One remained lit.

His unease was probably misplaced. He should go home. The hour drew late, and he'd not eaten yet. He got out of his car and headed to the door to her place, jogging up the single flight of stairs and pausing outside for a listen. He didn't press his ear. Nor did he knock. He cussed himself inwardly for being so weak and turned around. One foot hovered over the stairs to leave.

Go home.

What if she's in distress and no one knows?

He whirled and knocked before he could change his mind.

Tap. Tap.

No reply.

Perhaps she was in the bathroom.

Or on the floor with a brain bleed.

Kicking in the door seemed a little drastic, yet turning the knob showed the door locked. He eyed it and then reached into his pocket for his picks. A cop wasn't supposed to carry around those kinds of tools. Then again, most cops weren't also werewolves with an order from their Pack Alpha to keep Lycans from being discovered.

Click. Click. It didn't take long to turn the tumblers of the cheap lock—which he made a mental note to have replaced. A beautiful woman like Brandy should have something more secure. Look at how easily he opened the door and stepped inside.

Wham. The frying pan came out of nowhere.

Billy didn't go down, but he did cuss. "What the fuck?"

"Billy?" Brandy blinked at him, looking cuddly soft in some kind of Sherpa onesie with her hair damp and curly and smelling sweet from her shower. "What are you doing here?"

"Came to check on you. You know, in case you had a concussion or something."

"Do you always break into homes when doing a welfare check?"

"Why didn't you answer when I knocked?"

"Because I was in the kitchen making myself a snack. Popcorn, in case you're curious. I came out and heard someone fiddling with the lock, so I grabbed the nearest weapon." She waggled her pan.

"Next time, make it a knife. Or better yet, get yourself a baseball bat. You'll get better leverage while remaining out of reach."

"I'm thinking, given the way my day is going, I need a bodyguard. The live-in kind. Want to apply?" Her lips curved in invitation.

He almost said yes. "No need for anything that drastic. That druggie won't be back."

"Good. I knew you were the man to call. Popcorn?" She whirled from him rather than ask questions he'd rather avoid.

"No. I should go."

"Aren't you going to stick around, you know, in case I do have a concussion?"

Despite that being his fear, he argued, "You seem fine."

"For now. But for all we know, my brain is bleeding. Maybe you should hang for a bit. You know. Keep me awake. Or if I do fall asleep, make sure you poke me every few hours. I do love a good poke." She winked and then peeked downwards.

He cleared his throat and struggled to not have his body react. "If you're worried, I can drop you at the hospital."

"That doesn't sound like any fun," she opined over her shoulder. "I'd rather you were my nurse." She disappeared into her kitchen, and he heard the door of a microwave open and shut, followed by the rattle of popcorn being poured into a bowl.

He eyed the door. Escape. Probably the smartest thing he could do.

She emerged, looking adorably cuddly holding a giant bowl of popcorn, and he didn't need to sniff deep to notice she'd drizzled butter atop it as well.

"Wanna watch something?" she asked.

No. The correct answer was no. So why did he sit down?

The couch could have held three people easily, yet rather than sit opposite of the corner he'd chosen, she sat right beside him and then dared to place that bowl in his lap.

He stared at it as she said, "Now we can share."

Did she even realize what she did to him each time she stuck her hand into that bowl, sitting atop a groin with a hard-on? It was luckily contained, or it would have tipped over the popcorn.

He sat ramrod straight and unseeing. Could not have said what played on the screen.

A totally unaffected Brandy chattered by his side. "So that girl there, she's been taken in by the nuns, only she's not a nun, but she has some power that the demons want and—"

He breathed deep. Popcorn. Butter. Brandy. Brandy's arousal.

Oh fuck.

He'd known she was attracted to him—after all, the feeling was mutual—but he'd been doing his best to pretend. His best to ignore.

Just as he readied himself to rise and make his excuses to leave, he heard a tiny yowl and then a furball the size of his fist came out of nowhere and landed atop his head.

"Frou-frou!" Brandy squeaked as Billy bolted upright from the couch with the kitten on his head holding on for dear life with her sharp little claws while gnawing on his scalp. The popcorn bowl almost went flying. Brandy's fast reflexes saved it.

"Get it off!" he growled. Probably not the right tone to take with a feline reacting to a wolf being in her home.

Rather than come to his rescue, Brandy, her mouth rounded and her eyes sparkling, laughed. "Detective Gruff, anyone ever tell you how handsome you look wearing a pussy?"

Billy didn't blush. Ever. Tell that to the heat rising in his cheeks.

He reached up and scooped the feline terror and handed it to Brandy. "I gotta go."

He fled before he did something stupid, like seduce Brandy. But he had no escape when she seduced him in his dreams.

3

Brandy woke with a massive headache and would have hated life more if it wasn't Saturday. The clinic wasn't open on weekends. Time enough to recover and hopefully avoid an I-told-you-so from Maeve since she'd wanted to send over one of the boys from the pot shop to stay with Brandy.

Thinking of the pot shop... Her headache could use a bit of help from Mary Jane. Usually, she would walk over to her favorite store—Lanark Leaf, owned by Griffin Lanark, Maeve's sexy other half—but given she had connections, Brandy made a call.

"Ulric, I need you to promise you won't tell Maeve," she begged the moment he answered.

"Whoa. Before I agree, what's this about?" was his cagey reply.

"I might have had a run-in with an aggressive addict last night at the office—"

"What?" he bellowed.

"It's okay. It's been handled, but before I took his ass out, he might have slapped my head off a desk a couple of times, and now it is throbbing something fierce."

"I know exactly what you need," he growled. "Be there in twenty."

Ulric hung up, and Brandy collapsed on her couch after unlocking her door. Froufrou chose to curl up in a ball atop her left breast, but given her boobs were nice and squishy, she couldn't blame the kitten for using them as a pillow.

When Ulric arrived, he knocked once and walked in bearing a plastic grocery bag.

"Are those chips?" she asked, seeing the crinkly top of a familiar brand.

"Also got some of those donuts you like. A package of mixed chocolate bars. A bottle of orange juice and some cut-up watermelon."

She blinked. "Watermelon?"

"Because it's great for hydrating, full of nutrition, and, most of all, delicious, but first…" He dug into a pocket and extracted a brown bottle. "CBD oil. Best shit we've got in the store for headaches and other aches and pains."

"You are a god among men." She reached for it, which shifted her boob, resulting in little claws digging deeper. She winced.

Ulric chuckled. "I see the little terror has calmed down."

"Don't be fooled by her docile appearance now. At three o'clock in the morning, she sprang off the headboard onto my blanket to kill my foot because it moved," Brandy complained even as she smiled at the sleeping kitty.

While she took the prescribed dosage of oil, Ulric lay out the stash of food, even fetched her a glass and napkins. Only then did he say, "So, gonna tell me what happened? Maybe give me a description so I can hunt down the fucker that thought it was cool to smack you around?"

"It's already been taken care of. Billy gave me a hand."

Ulric's brows almost left his face. "You called the cops?"

"No, I called Billy," she clarified.

"Instead of me?" Ulric sounded insulted.

"Because you would have told Griffin, who would have told Maeve, and I didn't want her finding out, given she wasn't feeling so hot and already has so much on her plate what with the wedding in days. You know her, she would have tried to doctor me."

"And you think Billy won't tell Griffin?"

Brandy pursed her lips in reply. Given Billy was practically an outsider with his pack because of his job, she'd kind of assumed he'd be more close-mouthed.

"Maeve is going to be pissed you didn't tell her," Ulric remarked.

"I'm gonna tell her later, once she's Mrs. Lanark."

"Maeve's too modern to take his last name," Ulric opined.

"In some things, yes, but in this, she wants to leave her old name behind." Maeve bore her mother's last name, and given the lies she'd uncovered—mainly that her father wasn't dead, as her mother claimed, and had been helping financially as well as watching over her from afar—had her wanting a fresh start from the past. Especially since Maeve had reunited with her father.

"Well, shit. I'm gonna owe Quinn a favor. He bet me she would change it."

"What kind of favor?" she asked.

"The kind that came out with him sounding like a mobster." Ulric put on a flat expression as he muttered in a low rasp, "One day I'm going to ask you for help, and you won't say no."

"Maybe he's moving and needs some muscle for furniture?" Brandy suggested, starting to relax as the oil began to do its thing, easing the throb in her head.

"Oh no, it's going to be for something utterly insane. It will be like that time he dragged Dorian along on that trip to Asia."

"What happened?" Brandy asked.

"They've never spoken of it. But Dorian has an epic scar across his back."

"Haven't you ever wanted to adventure?"

Ulric rolled his big shoulders. "I guess. Ain't much to do around Ottawa, though."

Living in the city tended to fall into a routine that never changed. Get up. Go to work. See concrete when she was outside. Plaster and those glaring lights when in.

"Maybe it's time you took a trip. Head up north. Stay at a lodge or a cabin."

"Commune with nature?" He wrinkled his nose. "I'm surprised you of all people would suggest it."

"Meaning what?" she exclaimed. "I love the great outdoors."

"You just called it the great outdoors." He shook his head. "You are not a nature kind of woman."

"I have a plant." Brandy waved her hand in its direction.

"It's plastic."

"Still counts." An argument even she'd have a hard time defending. She really should try harder to get some green growing stuff around here. It was supposed to be a great way of filtering air.

"You wouldn't last one day up North," he opined.

"Would too!" Might as well keep lying.

"Only if you had some help. You know who's a great outdoorsman?" Ulric paused before saying, "Billy. You should see this place he bought. Acres and acres of forest."

"Really? Good for him." Brandy feigned disinterest

even as she wondered if said forest came with a cozy chalet and fireplace.

"How is Billy?" Ulric drawled. "Haven't seen him around much of late."

"Isn't it a good thing a cop isn't interested in your pot shop?"

"We're one hundred percent legit," Ulric argued. "Ain't no reason he can't be seen with us."

"Except for the fact he's not supposed to use it."

"Just because he hangs with Griffin doesn't mean he's smoking," he countered.

"What Billy needs is a reason why he can show up that has nothing to do with the pot. Pity he doesn't have a brother or cousin in there. Some kind personal connection with someone."

Ulric ribbed his chin. "Maybe he can pretend to be dating Quinn or me."

"You'd date Billy?" Her lips quirked.

"Yeah, that might be a hard sell given we're both into the ladies." And now that he'd laid the trap, Ulric looked less than innocent as he said, "If only we knew someone who could get close to Griffin without anyone being the wiser. Say, Griffin's fiancée's best friend."

"Me, date Billy?" Brandy huffed. "In a heartbeat, but he'll never agree to it. You should have seen his reaction when I asked him to be my plus-one at the wedding." She wasn't about to pretend she wouldn't like to be his girlfriend. For all that grumpiness, she saw the good guy underneath. Not to mention the attraction was insane.

"He said no?"

"Very emphatically."

The reply brought a grimace to Ulric's lips. "Guess I shouldn't be surprised. He's determined to never ever settle down."

"It was one date. Not a lifetime."

"Billy's a little rigid when it comes to personal connections."

"Why?" she asked.

"Let's just leave it a shitty childhood."

Rather than pry, she changed the subject. "I am craving the salt. All the salt. Chips, please." She held out her hands. The boob jiggled a bit too much, so kitty dug in four paws and teeth to tame it.

"Eek!" she squeaked.

Ulric laughed and saved her by crinkling the receipt in the treat bag, which drew Froufrou's attention. While the kitten pounced, Brandy shoved chips into her mouth. Don't judge. Some mornings called for comfort foods, like Ruffles Sour Cream 'N Bacon Chips. Salty. Crunchy. Delicious.

Like Billy.

Hmm. Blame the pot for that random thought.

"Whatcha thinking?" her big blond friend asked.

"I'm thinking that maybe someone could change the detective's mind. Perhaps suggest, discreetly of course, to accept my offer of going as my plus-one to the wedding."

"Why would you want to go with him when you could go with someone handsome like me?"

"Do you want to shag me?" Brandy asked in all seriousness.

Ulric made a lemon-sucking face. "You're like a sister to me."

"Exactly. You, Quinn, even Dorian. It would just be gross."

"But Billy isn't? Interesting..." drawled Ulric.

"If you're trying to make me say he's hot, then yes, he's like smokin'."

"You want me to set you up!" Ulric accused, only to immediately grin. "Holy shit. You and Billy. You think you've actually got a chance?"

"Yes." Brandy couldn't allow herself to doubt.

"He'll never agree. Like I said before, he is anti-relationship to the point he won't even buy the same bodywash twice in a row."

"Meaning, I should find someone else." Her nose wrinkled. "Do you know how long it took me to find Billy?" Apparently, with age came more discernment. She didn't want to be with just anybody.

"If Billy's your bar, maybe you should raise it."

"Not nice."

Ulric grinned. "Just kidding. Billy's a good shit. And he could use someone like you in his life. But if it's going to work, I'm going to need help. Is it okay if some of the boys give me a hand in convincing him?"

Her nose wrinkled. "Won't it backfire if Billy thinks you're ganging up on him?"

"We know how to be subtle." Ulric winked. "Trust me."

"I don't know..."

"Give me your phone."

"Why?"

"Because we're going to send him a message."

"We?" She arched a brow.

"Fine, then you send it."

"And say what?"

"Ask him to the wedding."

"I did. He said no."

"Because he didn't have time to think about it. Once he grasps the fact he can hang with us, I think he'll be open to the idea."

"He's stubborn. I doubt we can change his mind."

Ulric winked. "Don't worry. I've got an idea. Give me a few hours to introduce the idea to him and then text him again."

"You really think you can get him to change his mind?"

"Guess we'll find out."

Not exactly a ringing endorsement, but at the same time, she tingled with hope. Could Ulric convince Billy to go to the wedding with her? Even if Billy said yes, it didn't mean he'd want to actually date. What if he just wanted to pretend to be able to see his friends? Did it matter? She would have a chance to charm him into realizing he wanted her in his life.

Desperate? No. Brandy knew what she liked and, unlike some, wasn't afraid to put herself out there trying to get it.

After Ulric left, she chewed on some chocolate while she typed out a text. A careful one in case someone not in the loop read it.

Hey, Billy. Really enjoyed that coffee date we had last week, which is why I'm going to be bold and ask, what are you doing next Wednesday? My best friend is getting married, and I could really use a handsome date. What do you say?

She waited as long as her nerves could handle. Long enough she gnawed her thumb practically raw. When Ulric texted and asked if she had a date for the wedding, she took it as her signal. She sent the text to Billy.

He didn't reply that day. Sunday remained quiet too. It was late Monday before he replied with a simple, *Yes.*

4

Yes.

The moment Billy hit Send he wanted to take it back. What was he thinking? He couldn't go to the wedding with Brandy. The woman who already haunted too many of his thoughts and dreams.

No attachments. A vow he had no intention of breaking for a simple case of lust.

Blame his Pack. It started with Ulric slyly sending a message via their group chat on a private email server that said, *You know, if you dated someone close to Griffin or Maeve, you wouldn't have to sneak around.*

Not entirely true. If something were to happen and it were discovered Billy hung around with a drug dealer, even a legal one, he'd be in a sticky spot. His union may or may not protect his back. There was much stigma still attached to the marijuana trade. At the same time, the chance to actually be a part of the Pack tempted.

He remembered what if felt like to belong. Back in the day he'd been a regular at the ranch where Griffin spent his summers with his cousins. The foster family who took him in—a kind pair of older women, Lisette and Marie, who never had children of their own—had a knack for handling teenage boys. They lived next door to the Lanark brothers and their broods. Not all of them actual family. Apparently, the Lanarks were more interested in character than blood.

Later Billy understood just what that meant—and why on the full moons there was an inordinate amount of howling. He'd never been more humbled or happier than when he'd been asked to officially become a part of the family.

A family he'd had to more or less give up to become something he'd always wanted. A person who upheld the law and provided justice. Who helped others, especially his Pack brothers.

But what if he could help and also be a part of everything?

Quinn jumped into the conversation and said, *You can be my boyfriend.*

To which Billy replied, *Pretty sure your current girlfriend might have a problem with that.*

Being a smartass, Ulric just had to say, *Poly relationships are a thing these days.*

Griffin, being the alpha, did his duty by typing, *It's*

fine if Billy doesn't want to come to the wedding. I know he's got my back.

Fucker. Billy loved Griffin and really wanted to have his back in person.

Speaking of dates, Ulric posted, *who's picking up Brandy?*

Think she'll want to ride on the back of my bike? Surely Quinn wasn't serious?

She'll be wearing a dress and heels. She can hop in with me, Dorian offered.

As if she wants to be seen in your tiny-ass electric car, Ulric retorted. *I'll bring the Mustang out of storage so she can ride in style.*

The very idea of Brandy and Ulric together... It twisted his stomach something fierce.

Which was when Griffin jumped in again. *According to Maeve, she's riding with her in the limo. So no ride needed.*

The mention didn't ease his mind as much as he'd have liked. Because it still left her as a single woman at a wedding.

It was Ulric who suggested, *You know, going as her date doesn't mean you have to date for real. Just pretend, bro.*

Doesn't seem honest or fair to Brandy. Billy was big on trust.

Please. Brandy's a good sort. She'd totally be up for helping out a brother. Where do you think I got the idea?

Wait, had Ulric been discussing him with Brandy?

Griffin was the one to end the conversation. *This is Billy's choice.*

Totally right. And Billy wasn't the type to use someone. Brandy deserved better than a fake boyfriend. Not to mention, he worried that pretending would lead down the slippery slope where he wanted to make it real. No denying the spark between them.

A spark that wouldn't take much to ignite.

Avoid. He'd been doing a fine job of it, yet when she texted and asked him again to be her date, did he immediately reply with a negative? Nope. He hemmed. He hawed. He reminded himself over and over why it was a bad idea.

The inner struggle had him hesitating to type a reply to her invitation. He started tapping out a response. Erased it. Re-started.

He had a mental list of all the reasons he should say no. He refused to do the opposite about why he should say yes. He didn't want to be convinced. He really should stay away.

In the end, he couldn't resist.

He typed yes. He told himself it was because he wanted to be there for Griffin. The problem would be not letting things go too far. The last thing he wanted was for Brandy to get hurt.

Hell, he worried about himself, too. It would be all too easy to succumb to her allure, to forget his past, his promise to himself. His friends made it sound so easy.

It wasn't.

He was taking Brandy to a wedding. Fuck.

Because he couldn't be associated with the Pack, he had to rent his suit on his own from a different location, which took his measurements and then decked him out. Even he had to admit the store outfitted him better than his usual stuff bought off the rack. He cleaned out his car, vacuuming it and washing it before going to church. Brandy hadn't needed a ride, given she spent the night before and morning with the bride getting ready. But as her date, he'd be expected to see her home.

As Billy entered the church, he pretended to not know Ulric and uttered a loud, "Hi, I'm Billy Gruff. Brandy Herman's date."

"I finally get to meet the sexy detective she's been raving about." Ulric beamed as he slapped Billy on the back and ushered him inside.

"Sexy?" Billy snorted when they were past the threshold and any outside prying eyes.

His friend snickered. "Would you have preferred grumpy?"

"You're really making me rethink my decision to come."

"Relax. Enjoy yourself. You will have fun. Brandy's awesome."

"I'm surprised you're okay with this charade. I get the impression you're close." Billy tried to sound casual even as his ire for Ulric grew. Just how well did he and Brandy know each other?

"Bah, she's like the little sister I never had."

"She's older than you." A slip that raised Ulric's brow as it showed he'd been looking into her.

"Older maybe, but tiny in comparison. Which reminds me, as her unofficial big brother, I'm going to have to warn you to be nice, or I'll have to hurt you."

Billy grimaced. "If she wanted nice, she should have chosen another date."

"I agree. Not to mention she could have had someone cuter, like me," Quinn retorted, joining them.

"I thought you had a girlfriend."

"Not anymore. She started talking babies. I mentioned the big snip. And I am now single again, baby." Quinn winked.

Possessed by a sudden irrational urge to hit Quinn, Billy clenched his fist and, through gritted teeth, growled, "Don't you have people to usher?"

"Chill, bro. It's like you're not happy to be here."

"I'm ecstatic," was his flat reply. He was really second-guessing his choice to attend at the moment. While he'd been keen on seeing his good friend marry, he'd not realized how odd it would feel to be among them in the open. Usually, he had to sneak around to meet up with his Pack or go somewhere so remote no one would actually be able to see them.

Ulric held out his hand. "Let's get you seated. Since you're with Brandy, you get the bride's side."

The church held only a few people, as Maeve insisted on something small. She had only her father as family. As for Griffin, only the current Pack plus Uncle Bernard attended.

Billy didn't see Brandy anywhere in the church. Then again, didn't a maid of honor walk the aisle throwing flowers or something? This was actually his first wedding.

The pew proved hard, the choice of a church odd unless you knew Pastor Kyle was a werewolf, a loner who turned to God for a purpose. Given Pastor Kyle had been around since before Griffin became Alpha, he never made a fuss about it. Some other Pack territories didn't allow any unaffiliated Lycans at all.

People took their seats and the rustling settled as the music started. A song even he recognized.

He half turned to look like everyone else and then remained frozen as Brandy emerged first, holding a bouquet, wearing something in a dusky pink color that clung to her curves and dipped over her breasts. Her bare shoulders tempted. How he'd love to bite.

Blink.

He heaved in a breath. No bite. No matter how delicious she looked. Behind her, Maeve entered on the arm of her father, Russell, Alpha of the Toronto Golden Paw Pack.

This wedding wasn't just a happy day for Griffin. It actually formed an alliance with one of the most powerful packs in Canada, rivalled only by the one in Alberta.

Griffin looked so damned happy as Maeve joined him. The way he looked at her...

Billy's gaze slid sideways to Brandy. It clung to her, and what killed him was Brandy stared right back at him. And that smile? Why did her lips keep quirking in his direction? Why did it hit him like a bolt of lightning each time?

He had to fight her allure. He tried his best to focus on anything but Brandy. The actual couple getting married proved the easiest to fixate on. The ceremony went by in a whizz, with "I do's" exchanged, along with kisses. Then there was some whistling and a bit of howling as the new couple walked past, hand in hand. In a feat of fine planning, the reception was being held in a restaurant almost right across from the church.

Brandy didn't follow the newlyweds, rather she came to see him, her lips curved in a smile. "Looking sharp, Billy."

"You look nice too." He kept it tame. "Shall we go to the dinner?"

"In a second. I haven't said hello to the other boys yet." She sashayed across the aisle and was greeted with some whistles. His Pack brothers hugged her, made her laugh and smile. Not once did she look at him. Why should she?

She was supposed to be his date.

Billy almost reached for the gun he'd left home. He frowned. Why would he care if she talked to other men? She was allowed. After all, they weren't dating.

Tell that to his feet and his mouth. He marched across the floor to interrupt with, "Shall we head to the restaurant? I could use a predinner drink." One drink only since he'd be driving.

"Tequila time!" Ulric shouted.

People with secrets downing large amounts of alcohol seemed like such a bad idea. It was why initially Billy sat at the bar nursing a soda. Brandy had no such compunction. She dashed salt on her hand, licked it, sucked back a tequila shot, and then made the cutest face each time she sucked on her lemon slice.

He'd love to suck on her.

Whoa. He switched from cola to his one and only allowed beer just as their waiter told them their private dining room was ready. If by private they meant the space to the left of the bar reserved for their group. The right side held regular patrons.

The food came out in waves, and it might have been good. He couldn't taste it, given he was all too aware of the press of Brandy's leg against his.

The dinner came with wine, and the cousins also ordered pitchers of beer for the table. All of which Billy avoided.

Brandy gave at least two tipsy toasts, as did a few of the pack members. Billy would have loved to talk about the man he saw as a big brother who'd given him the one thing he always wanted, a family and a sense of belonging. However, he remained aware they were in a somewhat public setting and his role as Brandy's date meant he had to hold his tongue. Yet, while he couldn't speak, at least he could enjoy being present instead of hearing about it after the fact. How many things had he missed out on because he'd chosen to become a cop?

At the same time, he didn't regret the choice. He loved the job. Loved being able to help people. But at times, the demons of loneliness came to chew on him, making him wish he'd chosen a different path, one that allowed him to be a part of this all the time. But at the same time, he feared it. Billy didn't know how to be part of a family. Caring led to pain. Best to be alone where no one got hurt.

A maudlin thought to have in the middle of a celebration. Billy excused himself once to hit the head. He wished he could have more than the one beer, but he took his driving Brandy home seriously. He passed a boisterous table of guys and ignored the one who whistled.

When he exited the bathroom, centrally located for easy access by both sides of the restaurant, he would have ignored them once more, only one of them said, "That chick you're sitting with is fucking hot."

He cast a glance over his shoulder and stated flatly, "She's taken."

It felt better than it should have to declare it. Billy slipped back into the seat beside Brandy, who sipped at a frothy drink. She cast him a smile, her eyes shining, her laughter bubbling over. It seemed natural to drape his arm over the back of her chair. She leaned into him and fit in a way he rather enjoyed.

When Brandy excused herself to go to the washroom, he turned in his seat and watched her head into the tiny hall with the two bathrooms and an exit. The whistles didn't slow her one bit. A moment after she disappeared, two of the guys stood and glanced around first. One of them saw him watching and nudged the other. They shared a whisper and, with one last glance at him, went into the washroom area out of sight.

Could they look any more suspicious? He eyed the drink and recalled Brandy had been drinking tequila at first and then only wine. Why switch to something so sugary now?

He lifted the glass for a sniff.

"Since when do you drink girl mixes?" Ulric teased.

"Who ordered it?"

"Thought it was you, bro."

"Wasn't me." On a hunch, he took a sip. The sweetness didn't quite hide the hint of something else.

Oh fuck. He rose abruptly and made his way across the room. At his approach, the rest of the table from which the two had disappeared rose en masse to stand in his way.

He could have flashed his badge. It would have possibly dispersed them, but it would definitely lead to questions.

Billy tried defusing. "Excuse me."

"In a second, hamster bladder. Bathroom is full at the moment. Sit down and give it a few minutes."

The command arched his brow. "I don't think so. Move."

"Make us," was the belligerent reply.

He could have. Four guys? Tough, but not impossible, but he didn't want to be delayed. He lifted a hand. Just one. As if of one body, his brothers joined him at his back, outnumbering those he faced.

"You don't want to mess with us," hissed a fellow with pockmarked cheeks.

Griffin stepped forward, his tuxedo barely containing the physical presence of the alpha. "Actually, I'm the one you don't want to fuck around with. I just got married. And my wife's best friend is in that bathroom. Someone dear to everyone currently glaring at you, so move your ass, or I'm going rip it apart."

"We ain't interested in the woman."

"Then move. I won't ask again."

The music kept playing as the tension mounted. Even the bartender, who'd gone to college with Quinn, kept quiet. The chef was the one to emerge from the kitchen, snapping, "You miscreants are bothering my best customers. Out of my restaurant, or you'll find out what goes into my Sunday special."

"We're going," sulked the lankiest one.

"What about..." The youngest jerked his hairless chin in the direction of the bathroom.

The way they said it... Billy shoved past them and

charged into the women's bathroom. No Brandy. He whirled and saw no exit, not even a window. Emerging, he saw Ulric standing in the doorway of the men's room.

"Where is she?" he growled, about to push past.

"Not here, bro. Looks like those bozos just wanted privacy to do some snow." The cocaine was still on the counter, the two guys from the table pressed against the wall with wide eyes.

But no Brandy.

Suddenly anxious, Billy shoved against the bar on the third door with the exit sign over it. He emerged into an alley and saw a sagging Brandy being supported by some asshole wearing all black, headed for a car parked in the alley.

He didn't think; he reacted. Clothes exploded, fur sprouted, and he uttered a snarl as he suddenly raced for Brandy and her abductor.

The fellow turned his head, and suddenly there was a gun in his hand, and he fired off a few shots.

Billy dodged, glad the prick lacked aim. The fucker must have realized he was in deep shit, as he let Brandy go and she hit the ground in a boneless heap. The fucker then made a sprint for the car.

Oh hell no. Billy wasn't letting him get away. The man dove into the passenger seat, yelling, "Drive! There's a rabid dog chasing my ass."

That's wolf, fucker. As the car revved, Billy leaped. His front paws hit the trunk even as it slid away. It tore out of the alley and screeched as it turned onto the street. By the time Billy reached the sidewalk, it had raced out of sight.

Dammit. At least he'd had the forethought to memorize the plate. He trotted back toward Brandy. Ulric had already picked her up off the ground.

As Billy neared, Maeve emerged, despite Griffin saying, "Don't panic. Billy and Ulric are handling it."

If by handle he meant Billy lost the guy trying to kidnap Brandy.

"Brandy! Oh my god. What happened to her?" Maeve's first glance went to her limp friend. Then she caught sight of Billy in his wolf form. She pointed. "Whose dog is that? I don't see a collar or a leash. Don't let it get near her in case he's not friendly."

Griffin whispered to his wife, a whisper they all heard. "That's not a dog."

Her eyes widened. "Then who?" She glanced around before muttering, "Is that Billy? But there's no full moon."

"I'd say there were extenuating circumstances," Griffin replied.

No shit. Billy saw Brandy being kidnapped, and he didn't think; he reacted. Now the only problem was how to shift back. On the full moon, once shifted, usually a Lycan had to either exhaust themselves or wait out the night.

"And the white fur? That's not usual for these parts," Maeve murmured.

"Maybe talk about Billy's weird coloring another time. We might want to get back inside before the staff start talking." Ulric provided a voice of reason.

Griffin grimaced. "Good point."

"I am not going anywhere without Brandy," Maeve declared. "The restaurant won't care so long as we pay."

Quin volunteered. "I'll handle the bill and shit. I'll tell them the newlyweds got horny and the rest of us suddenly got an urge to go dancing."

"I'll give him a hand with the bill since I doubt his credit card can handle it," Wendell added.

"Actually, everyone but Ulric and Billy, for obvious reasons, get back in there. Have a few more drinks. Wendell, make it a big tip and apologize for me leaving abruptly with my new bride. If anyone asks about Brandy, tell them she had too much to drink and was taken home." As Griffin came up with a plan, Maeve checked on Brandy, lifting her eyelids, pressing her fingers to her wrist and neck to gauge her pulse.

Billy could only watch anxiously as Maeve muttered, "No difficulties breathing. Temperature seems fine. But she's definitely been drugged."

"How? She was with us the entire time," Griffin growled.

It was Ulric who said, "Someone sent her a drink from the bar."

"Pretty fucking ballsy to attempt to kidnap her right under our noses."

Actually, it was a slap in the face considering she should have been safe surrounded by the Pack. Billy had failed to keep her safe.

As if reading Billy's mind, Griffin muttered, "This isn't your fault, Billy. No one could have expected anything so brazen."

"So she'll be okay?" Ulric asked.

Maeve nodded. "Most likely she'll sleep it off. But she might wake disoriented. Possibly even puking, given the alcohol also in her system. I don't want her to be alone. I'll go."

Ulric protested. "Like fuck. I mean, no. I can handle one puking woman."

"Maeve, is that okay with you?" Griffin asked.

Her lips pressed. "Yes, but if she looks to be in distress at all, you call me."

"Yes, ma'am."

"Billy, you'll come with us to the shop. You can hide out there until your wolf goes back to sleep." Griffin handed out more orders.

Leave Brandy? He shook his shaggy head.

"I don't think he likes your plan. Given how he's practically lying on top of her, I'm going to guess he wants to stick close," a perceptive Maeve noted.

"That's fine. Billy can come with me and Brandy," Ulric suggested, and that met with Billy's approval. Someone had to keep an eye on the very handsome Ulric and be there to apologize to Brandy when she woke up.

"Shouldn't we grab Billy's things?" Maeve pointed at the shredded suit. There went his deposit.

"I'll get his stuff." Ulric began scooping scraps of fabric and found a wallet and phone.

Maeve snickered. "And I thought the Hulk was violent with clothes."

For a woman who'd not known of their existence a short while ago, she'd come a long way.

Griffin jangled Billy's keys. "I forgot he drove here."

"Awesome. We can avoid a taxi." Ulric went to swipe the keys, but Maeve snared them first.

"You've been drinking."

"Barely," Ulric claimed. "And with water in between. I ain't no spring pup anymore you know. I know how to pace."

Even Griffin agreed. "With his metabolism and size, he'd have to drink significantly more."

Maeve wasn't satisfied until she had him balance on one foot and close his eyes and do nose taps while reciting the alphabet backwards.

Maeve's father chose that moment to show his face in the alley. "Did I miss something while I was out getting smokes?" Cigarettes, a nasty habit, and yet only for the smell and taste. Lycans oddly didn't get lung cancer like humans.

Maeve made a moue. "Someone tried to kidnap Brandy."

"Seriously?" The other alpha almost lost his eyebrows in surprise.

"Yeah. They roofied her and tried to snag her when she hit the head," Ulric explained.

Russell eyed Billy "I am going to guess he can't change back?"

He shook his head.

"Don't worry. An adrenaline shift usually wears off within a day or so. Get some sleep."

Griffin frowned. "Usually? So you've seen this before? I've only ever heard of it. This is my first actual case."

"Because it's rare."

"What if Billy doesn't change back. Then what?"

"Full moon might do the trick. If not, I've got a recipe we can try, but I warn you, having seen the ingredients, I predict it tastes like literal shit," Russell declared.

Billy grumbled.

"Here's to hoping we don't need it," Griffin added. "Ulric, get going and be sure to text at once if anything changes."

"It's your honeymoon night," Ulric reminded.

"Remember the chat we had the last time you didn't tell me about Brandy?" Maeve glared at Ulric until he shifted uncomfortably.

"I'll call. Jeez."

With that, Ulric picked up Brandy and, with a big hairy wolf by his side, carried her to the parking lot and

Billy's car. Billy rode with her in the backseat, a cushion for her limp body. When they arrived at her place, Ulric let him out first, muttering, "Make sure the coast is clear."

A quick scout up and down the block showed no one out and about at this hour. Only when he returned to the car did Ulric scoop Brandy up and carry her upstairs with Billy right on his heels.

Ulric was gentle about laying her on the bed. Billy had no problem with him removing her heels and even unpinning her hair, but when he rolled her over to start loosening clothes, Billy growled.

"Easy, friend. Was just trying to make her comfortable." Ulric held up his hands.

An only slightly mollified Billy crept close to Brandy and lay beside her, watching.

"Guess I'm getting the couch," Ulric complained.

A lift of Billy's wolf lip had Ulric arching both brows. "I ain't leaving."

Billy lay his head on her stomach and continued staring.

"Maeve told me to stay, and she's the alpha's wife and a shit-ton scarier than you. I'll be on the couch if you need me."

Ulric left, and after an hour of watching Brandy sleep peacefully, Billy finally slipped into slumber himself.

And had the best dream because she was in it.

5

Brandy woke pasty-mouthed in her bed, which, for some reason, she shared with a massive dog. Last thing she remembered was partying at Maeve's wedding dinner. The wine flowed freely along with tequila shooters. A lot of them, which Brandy kept downing. However, her recollection of things after dessert was served got a little hazy.

Apparently, she'd hit an animal shelter and adopted another pet. The big lump of fur didn't move at all when she shoved out from under its heavy paw.

At least she still wore her dress and panties, meaning she hadn't gotten too freaky. Still, a wolfish-looking dog in her bed? Good thing it wasn't a full moon, or she'd have assumed something else. The Lycan thing had been explained to her by Ulric and Quinn. According to them, non-alphas required a full moon to shift.

I wonder what possessed me to adopt a dog, though? Especially once as massive as this one.

She stood, and to her surprise, she noticed Froufrou, her kitten, sleeping tucked against the massive beast. A good sign? Or the calm before the wolfdog made her kitty its snack?

A visit to the bathroom left her bladder empty, and when she emerged—her wrinkled dress stripped in a favor of a long, voluminous robe—the wolfdog had disappeared. In its place, a naked man sprawled across her bed. And a nice one at that.

Bleary eyes opened and widened at the sight of her.

"Good morning!" she chirped. "Although it would be better with some coffee and Tylenol. It seems I had a few too many last night, because I don't remember anything after the crème brulé, although, given I was cuddling a wolf when I woke, I'm going to assume we did it doggy style." A joke, but how did he respond?

"I gotta go." The naked hunk literally dove off the bed and bolted from her bedroom.

He'd be back. After all, he lacked pants, and even if he did manage to escape, Brandy knew where Detective Billy Gruff worked.

Only Billy didn't go far. She emerged into the living room to find Ulric stretching on her couch wearing only a pair of shorts. Impressive, but she was much more interested in Detective Gruff's physique.

Tight and toned. Yummy, even if Billy scowled at the sight of Ulric. "You're still here?"

"Good morning to you, too, Detective Grumpy," Ulric drawled. "How'd you sleep?"

Rather than reply, Billy had a demand. "I need clothes."

"Don't get dressed on my account," Brandy teased as she sauntered past Billy, who had his hands cupping his groin. She ogled his tight ass—debated slapping it—before entering her tiny kitchen, where she almost died, as Froufrou dashed between her legs ready for breakfast.

The frantic meowing of her poor starving feline took precedence, and only once her furball had its face buried in a bowl of stinky wet food did she drawl, "Anyone need coffee?"

"Hell yeah," Ulric exclaimed.

"Great. There's a coffee shop across the street. I'll take a large, three sugar, one cream, and whatever pastry of the day they're offering." Brandy placed her order to a jaw-dropped Ulric. She smiled and added, "Thanks."

"Nicely played," the big man chuckled as he grabbed his shirt and pulled it on, followed by his pants. He glanced at Billy. "Anything for you?"

"Clothes."

"You got a spare set in your car?"

Billy nodded. "In the trunk. Not sure where my wallet and shit went."

"Phone and wallet are on the counter." Ulric dangled the keys he snared. "Back in a few."

Ulric left, and Brandy leaned against a wall as she said, "So, care to fill in the blanks from last night? 'Cause while I've done many wild things in my time, I've never come home with two guys before."

"There was some trouble at the restaurant."

"Trouble as in?" she questioned as he hesitated.

"Someone spiked your drink and then tried to abduct you," he blurted out.

Not the answer she expected. Her mouth rounded. "It was that pina colada, wasn't it? I guess it wasn't you that ordered it for me." That had been the only reason she'd drunk the frothy mix.

He shook his head. "Wasn't me. And they almost got away with you."

Her lips pursed. "Did you get them?"

"No." A disgruntled reply. He glanced around and spotted the afghan hanging over her couch. He snared it and wrapped it around his waist.

"What happened? Details please, because I don't remember anything." Not being kidnapped, saved, or how she'd ended up in bed with Billy the wolf.

"We interrupted before some guy could stuff you into a car driven by a second person."

"I can't believe they got away." Her lips turned down.

"They did. Which reminds me, I think I remember the plate number."

"Think?" She snorted. "Knowing Dorian if there was a camera anywhere in that area, he's already got it and checked." Griffin's tech fellow could get into databases not available to the public.

"Why don't you seem more freaked out?" he asked.

"Because I honestly don't remember much." She shrugged. "And you forget, this isn't my first kidnapping. But it is the second time you've come to my rescue. My hero."

Discomfited, he shifted uncomfortably. "Can you hand me my phone?" He only came close enough to hold out his hand, and no farther.

She grabbed it from the counter and dropped it into his open palm "You still haven't explained how you ended up in bed with me and how you were a wolf. I thought only Griffin could change without a full moon."

"According to what Russell said last night, it was caused by adrenaline."

"Why, Billy Gruff, were you worried about little ol' me?" She batted her lashes. "My hero."

He grimaced. "I would have saved anyone in the same situation." He downplayed it, and she might have been more miffed except for the fact she'd learned enough about Lycans to know his excuse didn't match his actions. Otherwise, there'd be a lot more wolf sightings.

"And the fact you slept in my bed?"

"Just wanted to stick close in case you woke up not feeling too good."

"Holding my hair while I heaved required you and Ulric?"

"Ulric wouldn't leave." A tight reply. "But enough of the fact I slept over. We should talk about who would want to kidnap you."

"No one?" She shrugged. "Maybe it was a mistake. I mean it's not like I'm some cute young thing that can be sold on the black market as a sex slave."

"You're plenty attractive."

"Be still my beating heart. I do believe that was almost a compliment."

Once more he scowled. "Just the truth. But I doubt that was the intent. For one, it was awfully brazen to come after you like that while surrounded by friends."

"And yet they almost got away with it," she pointed out.

"Do you have any enemies?"

"Carrots."

At his blank expression, she explained. "I'm allergic to carrots. Those little orange bastards make me break out in hives."

"I meant actual enemies, people who might have a grudge. Ex-boyfriend?"

"Only one crazy ex and he's not a problem anymore." Heck, she'd not thought of Clive in years. Creepy fucker was behind bars where he belonged.

"Maybe someone's wife or partner has a jealousy vendetta?"

His line of questioning made her laugh. "Are you accusing me of being someone's mistress?"

"Are you?"

"No. As a matter of fact I've not really dated much in the last year or so. The only ex I have that might have been capable of pulling that kind of stunt has been in jail for a while."

"Name?"

"Did you miss the part where he's in jail?" Where he belonged.

"It doesn't hurt to check it out."

"Go ahead. And while you're at it, check on your ex-girlfriends too. Maybe one of them has been stalking you and went into a jealous rage when they saw you were my date."

"It had nothing to do with me."

"Says you."

"Yes, says me," he snapped.

"I thought a good detective investigated all angles."

"We do, but that's a waste of time. I don't do relationships."

"Why not?"

His lips pressed into a tight line, and the chance to poke him harder disappeared as Ulric returned bearing the ambrosia of gods. Coffee and a cherry cream cheese pastry.

Mmm.

Billy took the knapsack Ulric brought back with him and went into her bathroom to change. He emerged wearing too many clothes.

"I should get going," he stated.

"Not worried my kidnapper will come back and try again?" she taunted.

Billy held up his phone. "No, because, according to Dorian, the car we saw last night was stopped early this morning and its driver is in custody."

"Ooh. Who is it?"

"Don't know but I'm going to go find out. You coming?" he asked Ulric.

"You gonna let me sit in on the interrogation?" Ulric's expression brightened. "I call good cop."

"You aren't coming to the precinct. I'm going to drop you off on my way so that Brandy can have some privacy."

"Oh, I don't mind if Ulric stays." The look Billy shot her warmed her right down to her toes.

"Ulric's leaving, aren't you?" Billy directed his words at the big man.

"Guess I should. After all, how would it look if your boyfriend left and I stayed?"

"I'm not her boyfriend," Billy growled.

"What happened to being pretend lovers? Don't tell me we're already breaking up," Brandy teased.

She'd have sworn Billy uttered a guttural animal sound before spitting through gritted teeth, "I'll check in on you later. Lock the door. Don't answer unless you know who it is, and even then, text me if you do."

"Oooh, look at you, giving me orders like we really are a couple." Brandy followed the men as they headed for the door.

Ulric exited first, but Billy paused on the threshold. "Just because we arrested someone doesn't mean you shouldn't be careful," he admonished.

"You're adorable when you're protective," she replied.

"I'm being serious."

"But what if I want you to be my hero again? After all, you are really good at the rescue thing."

"Only because I've been able to arrive in time."

"Then maybe you should stick closer to me."

His nostrils flared. "I don't think that's a good idea."

"Why? Afraid you won't be able to fake it? Let's find out, shall we?" Before he could say anything, she lifted on her tiptoes to brush a kiss over his mouth. He stilled, a rigid statue who didn't respond until she whispered, "If this ruse is going to work, then it's got to be believable."

It led to one arm coming around her and dragging her closer. His mouth slanted over hers for a hard kiss, and he muttered, "Don't do anything stupid."

"No promises," she said as Billy left, casting her a dark glance over his shoulder that left her smoldering.

Damn but that man was too sexy for his own good.

Still, despite all her teasing, she did take caution and locked her door. When a knock arrived less than a minute later, though, she flung it open assuming he or Ulric forgot something.

Instead, Maeve walked in with a baffled expression. "What did you do to poor Billy? He peeled out of here like he was being chased by a flock of geese."

"I resent being compared to an avian terrorist." Canadian geese were no joking matter.

"At least he was back to himself this morning. That was a surprise, seeing him changed like that last night."

"I'm just glad Griffin told you about the whole Lycan thing before you guys got married, or that would have been awkward to explain." She'd been vocal with him about not keeping it a secret. Griffin had been scared to say anything, given how his own mother had reacted. However, in the end, he didn't want to start his life with Maeve on a lie.

"I still can't believe I married a werewolf." Maeve giggled. "Sounds like the title of a romance novel."

"Actually, I think I read that story…" Brandy had devoured dozens in her quest to understand.

"I wonder why his wolf was white furred, though. You'd think with his dark hair, his pelt would match."

Brandy's lips pursed. "Good question." She'd have to ask Billy when he returned—if he returned.

"How are you feeling?" Maeve asked. "You're looking recovered from the drugging last night."

Brandy's nose wrinkled. "Feeling fine, if stupid. I

can't believe I didn't question where that drink came from. I'm usually more careful."

"In your defense, it was pretty darned brazen. I'm just glad you're okay." Maeve hugged Brandy.

"I might be fine, but what about you? What are you doing here? You're supposed to be on your honeymoon."

"Griffin rescheduled our flight for later so I could pop in and check on you before we left. Good thing I did, given Billy and Ulric abandoned you."

"Billy didn't give Ulric a choice."

"Sounds like your fake boyfriend has jealousy issues."

"I should be so lucky." Brandy giggled. "Seriously, one minute he's saving me from being kidnapped and sleeping in my bed, and the next, he can't escape fast enough."

"Wait, he slept with you?"

"Yes, and probably left a ton of wolf hair on my sheets. Nothing happened," she hastened to add at Maeve's dropped jaw.

"You sound disappointed."

Because she was. "If it's meant to be, it will happen."

After all, if there was one thing she'd learned from reading werewolf romance, when it came to mating, you couldn't fight fate.

And Brandy was pretty sure Billy was meant to be her wolfman.

6

Billy couldn't get away from Brandy's place fast enough. He barely touched the brakes as he whipped around a corner.

"Damn, man, what are we escaping?" Ulric put a hand on the dash to brace himself.

"Just driving. Why you acting like a pussy?" He deliberately antagonized Ulric to avoid admitting to himself he was fleeing as if terrified.

With reason.

Brandy scared the living fuck out of him.

Wait, not accurate. How she made him feel was the most terrifying thing, not the woman herself.

"I am comfortable enough in my masculinity to not give in to your toxic male attitude and admit I'd like to arrive alive."

Billy started laughing, and a good thing he had a red light to stop for so he could full out chuckle. "That is priceless coming from a guy who used to dirt bike in Death Gorge."

"I've chosen to be less reckless with my life as I age."

"Age?" That caused Billy to snort as the light turned green and he hit the gas, not as hard as before. "We're barely halfway through our lives."

"Don't remind me." Ulric's lips turned down.

Don't ask him. Don't ask him. He told himself not to and still blurted out, "You okay?" An intimate question to ask of someone he'd known a while but not as well or as intimately as some of the others in the Pack, like Griffin.

"I'm good but for the fact I can't meet the right woman."

Billy coughed. "You're moping about your lack of love life?"

"Yup. I want to find Mrs. Right. Apparently I don't know where to look."

This kind of revelation threw Billy for a loop. "When you least expect it, you'll meet and bam."

Ulric glanced at Billy as he slowed for another red light. "You speak like you've experienced it. Is it someone I know?" A sly query.

Don't move. Don't react. Billy cleared his throat. "I'm never settling down, you know that." He'd seen firsthand what happened to love. It started hot and exciting then turned into a toxic spiral that kept repeating over and over. It surprised him that more people didn't avoid entanglements in the first place.

"I'll bet that you will fall hard. So fucking hard that I would wager money on it."

"How much?" Billy asked. "Hundred bucks?"

Ulric snorted. "Don't be ridiculous." He paused. "I will wager that motorcycle you've been working on in your garage."

"Are you insane? It's worth thousands."

"And? The whole point of a wager is confidence. If you really believe you won't fall in love and get mated, then wager it. Right now."

His mouth went dry. His heart raced. The answer on the tip of his tongue. He shook his head. "You're being insane. I can't bankrupt you like that when I win."

"You are so going to fall in love," Ulric sang. "It's like you're waving a red flag in front of fate. I am going to enjoy this."

"I'm not wagering because it's dumb," Billy growled.

"Sure you're not. You're not worried at all about falling for Brandy."

"You're insane. I am not interested in Brandy."

"Do you cuddle a lot of women in surprise wolf form?"

He pursed his lips. "That was an accident."

"If you say so." Ulric then asked innocently but pointedly, "You ran away awfully fast from Brandy back there. Is something going on I should be aware of?"

Don't fucking squirm. He kept his eyes on the road as he said, "I told you about the message Declan sent. I've got to get to the precinct."

"If in such a rush, why drag me along? I could have caught my own ride."

Billy turned and headed up a new road with less traffic. "Dropping you off is only a detour of a few minutes."

"Says the guy who usually avoids being seen with me."

"That was before you convinced Brandy to be my fake girlfriend."

"You're welcome. You have to admit it's a brilliant way to see you more publicly."

"I might still get fired for hanging out with a dealer and his crew."

"Then you get fired and you turn into a PI or personal security specialist."

"You have it all figured out."

"More like I've thought of it. Miss hanging with you, brother."

Billy huffed out, "Me too." Ulric had been a part of his college life and he'd gotten to know Griffin because of him. Brothers of fraternity turned brother wolves.

"Just think of how awesome it would be to hang out more. I'm already over at least once a week for dinner with Brandy. She kicks my butt at virtual bowling."

Billy slammed on the brakes, and Ulric snapped forward. "Whoa, dude. I thought we were done with the killing thing. What's the matter? Jealous?"

"No," he muttered through a tight jaw.

"So, the fact I'm going to swing by her place again around lunch to check on her doesn't bother you one bit."

"Nope." His hands clenched the steering wheel so tight he worried it might snap.

"Good to know. So, about the guy the cops arrested, you got any extra details? Like why they even stopped him? I wouldn't have thought Griffin would have let Maeve file a police report."

Billy shook his head. "The car was pulled over because it was reported stolen." That had been in the message he'd gotten from the chief herself as he left Maeve's place. It asked him to swing by ASAP.

"Do you always get called in about grand theft auto? I thought you worked the guns and gang crime stuff."

"Usually, but apparently the guy they took into custody is refusing to talk to anyone but me."

"Meaning he knows you."

Billy shrugged. "Maybe. I wasn't given a name or a picture. Guess I'll soon find out."

"You sure I can't tag along?"

"And how would I explain that to my chief?"

Ulric grinned. "Maybe I could be your informant."

"Or maybe you could let me do my job." He pulled

to a stop outside a popular fast food chain restaurant. "Here's where you get out."

"But my place is still like three blocks east."

"Your legs work."

"You suck," Ulric grumbled as he stepped out of the car into a lightly falling rain.

"Nice to see you too." Billy peeled away, drumming his fingers on the steering wheel. He'd not appreciate Ulric's line of questioning at all. Accusing him of liking Brandy. Or implying she was the one for him.

No.

Way.

And he wouldn't spend any time thinking about Brandy. Instead, he should think about what he'd be facing at the precinct and the strange fact his chief had been the one to text him: *Got a perp in custody. Will only talk to you.*

So weird and yet that didn't stop him from hitting his apartment first to have a quick sluice and change his clothes. While this was supposed to be a day off, he couldn't exactly ignore a message from his boss. He parked in the employee lot, went inside, and greeted his coworkers. A tilt of his head, a wave of his hand, a low toned, "Hey."

He left the more public areas for his assigned cubicle. It held nothing personal unless the chipped mug from the dollar store counted. He sat down and typed his password, the screen flashing from the log-in page to the desktop, where his messaging icon showed a few new ones. Before he could click and start reading, the chief entered the area and strode right for him.

He stood, "Chief."

"My office, please." She strode past him and expected him to follow.

The chief, an Asian woman of almost fifty years who'd been with the force for thirty, had shocked many who'd been used to having men in charge. Especially since she'd been head hunted from out of province. But Chief Bonnet knew how to run a tight precinct, and when she barked, people listened.

"Have a seat, Detective." She sat behind her desk. "I know you must have read my text by now or you wouldn't be here."

"I did. What do we know? Your message didn't say much, and I didn't have a chance to read anything else."

"It's an odd situation. We received a call last night about a stolen car. Early this morning, the vehicle was located and the driver arrested. Turns out he's in our system." She flipped her monitor around to show him the screen. "Harold Brunner. Sound familiar?"

The name hit Billy with surprise. "Is that the same Harold Brunner I busted for gun smuggling? Didn't he go to jail?"

She nodded. "He went but not for long. Given overcrowding, non-violent offenders were offered early release. He got out about a week ago."

"And has already been arrested for car theft?" At

times it was as if career criminals wanted back in the clink.

"Not exactly."

"But you said he was driving a stolen car."

"Reportedly stolen." The chief paused for a moment before saying, "It's registered to Harold Brunner."

He blinked. "I'm confused."

"So were we once we figured it out. See, when we pulled him over, we didn't know who he was. He wouldn't provide a name or any identification, so they brought Brunner in and charged him with auto theft. It was only during processing that we realized he already existed in the system and from there discovered the car belonged to him."

"Meaning the car wasn't stolen. So why haven't you let him go?"

"Because he won't leave. From the moment the cops arrested him, he's been demanding to talk to you."

"Why?" It made no sense. It had been years since he'd dealt with the man. Unless...Had Brunner also been behind Brandy's attempted kidnapping?

"We don't know. We told him he was free to depart, and he is refusing until he gets to speak with you."

"Is this about whoever reported his car stolen? Does he expect us to find the person who pranked him?" Billy treaded a fine line between asking the right questions while not revealing his possible earlier run-in with Brunner. Assuming it was him, why had the convict gone after Brandy? Billy could only assume it had to do with their prior run-in, a revenge thing so to speak.

"That's what you need to find out. Ask at the desk. Lorraine will tell you what room he's in."

Billy left the chief's office and wondered how he could get Brunner to leave. If he was involved in the Brandy thing, then the man needed to be handled away from the watching eye of the police. But he couldn't exactly toss the guy out. His chief would have even more questions if he did.

Maybe Brunner just wanted to cuss him out for having him arrested. Could be the Brandy thing was unrelated?

Even he didn't believe that. But that would mean being very careful. Entering the interrogation room, Billy had to remain aware of the one-way glass and two cameras taping his every move and word.

He couldn't let anything slip. If Brunner said something about Brandy, he'd have to play it off as well as he could. The man was dead. He just didn't know it yet, and it was his own fault. Brunner should never have tried to kidnap Brandy. Now he posed a danger.

Billy walked into the interrogation room to find Brunner looking much like before, gaunt and greasy looking. His hair was long and unwashed. He stank of cigarettes and wore a smirk.

"If it isn't the detective that busted my ass. About time you showed up."

"Hey, Brunner. Gotta say I feel pretty special, going through all that trouble just to chat. It's gonna cost a fortune to get your car out of impound."

"Keep it. I don't need it." Brunner hadn't lost his happy face.

"You know, you could have just called me."

"Ain't no fun in that. I wanted to see you when I delivered my message."

"And what message would that be?" Billy tried to not give anything away as he waited for a reply.

"That you should not have gotten involved in his business."

"Whose business?"

"*His*," Brunner replied with a grin more frightening than happy.

"If you're just going to waste my time—" Billy started to rise.

Brunner muttered, "I ain't finished saying my piece."

Billy remained in the room but didn't sit down. "Not really interested in anything those lying gums of yours want to flap. As far as I'm concerned, the parole system made a mistake letting you loose."

"They didn't have a choice. It was all part of the deal."

"What deal?" he asked, all too aware someone listened. It meant he couldn't lunge across the table, grab hold of Brunner, and shake him while demanding to know why the fuck he went after Brandy.

"The one *he* offered."

The reverent way Brunner said it gave some cause for worry. People who felt strongly about a leader could be unpredictable. A pack threatened would have to reply with discreet, yet deadly force.

"What's this supposed message for me?"

"You will pay for what you've done to him."

"A name would really help because I've done lots of things to many people."

"He is—"The fire alarm whooped, and Brunner stood. "That's my cue to go."

"Oh no you don't." Billy stepped close to Brunner and then, low enough that the microphone shouldn't pick it up over the siren, growled, "Why did you go after that woman last night?"

"Because he told us to."

Before Billy could shake him until he spilled a name, the door opened and Sergeant Markol barked, "Everyone out. Chief's orders." Markol's gaze flicked to Brunner. "Do we need to cuff him and put him with the other prisoners?"

Much as Billy would have loved to throw Brunner behind some bars, he had no cause. Besides, he'd prefer Brunner be set loose because then when he captured him later for questioning no one would be the wiser.

"Mr. Brunner is not under arrest," Billy stated as Brunner rose.

"I'm a free man, mother fucker. Free to do whatever I want, to whomever I want." The last was directed at Billy, who clenched his fists rather than punch the fucker in the mouth.

Later. Later Brunner would get what was coming to him.

And before anyone judged, for a long time Billy had followed the law, and look what happened? Over and over again, irredeemable pieces of shit were let loose on the world to terrorize good folk. It needed to stop. Especially now that Brandy had been threatened because Brunner wanted revenge on the cop who busted him.

Given the way his priorities were shifting, it might be time to rethink his career.

Billy remained a few paces behind the man as the joined the flow of people emerging into the blaring chaos comprising the reception area. While most people walked to the doors—unrushed because of the many previous false alarms—one fellow walked in with a duffel bag. Billy wanted to ignore it. Someone would have to be insane to try anything here with all the cops around. Insane or suicidal. Dammit. Billy shifted his direction, only to realize Brunner also headed straight for the guy with the bag.

Uh-oh.

The guy with the duffel reached inside and someone screamed, "He's got a gun!"

Indeed, a shotgun emerged in one hand, a revolver

in the other. Brunner took an outstretched weapon and pivoted in Billy's direction.

People screamed and stampeded, clearing a line of sight between Billy and Brunner.

As Brunner pulled the trigger, Billy ducked. Brunner kept firing and thankfully missing as Billy dove over the reception desk and hid behind with Pollard and Higgins.

There was distinctive shotgun blast then the pow of service revolvers as the cops in the room took care of the threat.

When the shooting stopped, Billy rose, doing his best to ignore the shrieking to his left to focus on the bodies on the floor. Two only. Brunner and his accomplice. He didn't see any other immediate casualties.

The clanging alarm kept going, but those left inside ignored it as they limped out of the spots where they'd taken shelter to regroup.

The chief came to stand by his shoulder. "What the hell just happened, Gruff?"

"I don't know. In the room, he alluded that someone had put him up to it."

"Who?"

"I never found out." Eyeing the bodies on the floor, he couldn't help disgruntlement, knowing he might never know the answer.

7

Brandy heard about the incident when she went down to grab a few grocery items. Apparently, two psychos pulled out some guns in the police station and started shooting. Given the amount of gunfire, it was a miracle only the psychos died. Everyone else escaped with minor injuries. That reassurance didn't stop her from texting Billy.

You okay?

No reply

Don't make me come down to that police station looking for you!

The response arrived quicky. *Am fine.*

Do you need a nurse?

No.

Are you sure? And because she could be a brat, she attached a picture of herself at a Halloween party wearing an indecently exposing nurse's uniform.

To her surprise, she got a wide-eyed emoji reply.

You coming over later? she asked, not knowing yet if last night's wedding date was a one-off.

The reply took a minute. *Maybe. Depends on how long I'm stuck here.*

He didn't say no. Oh hell yeah.

But it wouldn't be for a few hours by the sound of it. Plenty of time to check on the office. Get some wine. And make sure her shaved bits survived. She'd plucked and waxed for the wedding.

The walk to the building with their new practice didn't take long. It would be closed during Maeve's honeymoon. But if all went according to plan, and they expanded to share the office, they'd be able to rotate and have someone available at pretty much all times.

One of the first people they'd hire was Boris, Uncle Bernard's son, who was completing his medical residency. He was the only son who'd never shifted despite getting bitten more than once. Meanwhile his brothers all changed right away.

Brandy had so many questions about the whole biting-and-Lycan thing. Some of which the men couldn't answer. Like why not take men when they were older and their baby-making years past them instead of sterilizing them young? What happened to their sperm when they changed? Did they have a written history, or was everything orally handed down, making it susceptible to the telephone effect?

The sidewalk outside the office had a fair amount

of foot traffic this time of day, meaning it was easy to remember to lock the door after she got inside. She even rearmed the alarm system.

Despite the office being closed, emails and faxes kept arriving and could be daunting if not handled. One by one, Brandy sorted messages, called people to make appointments, and dealt with the many requests.

She left the email with its blank subject line for last. More from the creepy spammer.

Won't be long now. Sent the afternoon of the wedding. Made her think of the attempted kidnapping. Could it be her stalker took things too far?

Might be time to tell Billy about the emails.

She printed out the latest message and then went into her trash folder to move the others into a secure location and then sent them to the printer as well.

It might just be a coincidence—said every girl killed after feeling uncomfortable. Better embarrassed than sorry.

Bang. Bang. Bang.

The rapping at the door snapped her head up, but she didn't answer.

The clinic was closed. A great big sign in the door stated it.

Bang. Bang. Bang. The hard knocking rattled the door in its frame. The smoked glass held.

Brandy had time to hunt out a better weapon than her new computer monitor. The ironically named Billy stick, which she'd picked up from the security store, filled her sweaty palm.

Right about now, she really wished Maeve wasn't so adamant about no cameras where the patients could be filmed. Privacy concerns, blah blah. What about protection for the employees?

She held her phone in her free hand and thought about who to call. Billy came first to mind. The man made an excellent knight in grumpy-cop armor. However, he was busy what with that shooting at the station, and what if she only had a chance to make one call?

Tap. Tap. Tap.

The light knocking didn't ease her mind, but hearing Ulric bellow, "Yo, Brandy, you in there?" had her rushing to unlock the door, mostly so she could yank the man inside then berate him.

"What is wrong with you, scaring me like that?"

"I barely knocked," he exclaimed.

"Barely? The whole door was rattling. Didn't it occur to you after the first time you were pounding that doing it harder the second wouldn't work either?"

He stared at her. "What are you talking about? I just got here."

A chill clenched her stomach. "Don't mess with me."

"I'm not. Dorian said someone with your credentials logged into the computer, so I popped over to keep an eye on you."

"So that wasn't you knocking super hard twice before that pussy tap?"

He shook his head. "But probably a good thing you didn't answer."

She pursed her lips. "I highly doubt it was anything nefarious. Probably someone impatient to see a doctor." They got more than an entitled few every week who seemed to think their ailment should allow them to skip the others in line before them.

"Yeah, well, can't be too safe. You won't always have Billy around to rescue you. Damn that boy was something to see. I thought he was going to start tossing people left and right to get to you."

"Are we talking about the same Billy who ran away?"

"Only 'cause you're getting to him."

She snorted. "I highly doubt that. Speaking of whom, he might be popping by later, but he didn't say what time. Wanna pick up some Chinese with me? Then if he does, I'll have decent leftovers to heat up." And if he didn't, lunches for the rest of the week.

"You and Billy got a date?"

"Maybe." His text certainly implied it.

But she should have known Billy would ruin things.

8

Despite the hours of paperwork required after an active shooting involving fatalities, Billy was glad that Brunner and his friend were in a morgue instead of plotting their next kidnapping attempt on Brandy. The car they'd seized? A search of the trunk showed rope, masking tape, a ball gag, and a bottle of something that he'd wager was what they'd slipped into her drink.

And he had no doubt they would have tried again because the two dead men had a personal vendetta against him. It surely wasn't a coincidence that Billy recognized Brunner's partner, Sal Koover. Another crook he'd put away.

The question being was, had Koover been the one Brunner referred to as *he*? Or did Billy have to worry about another person still in the wings? At the same time, who would someone like Brunner be willing to die for? A man like him was usually only out for himself.

All these questions needed answer but most of all, he wanted to know if Brandy might still be in danger. A danger caused by him.

They wanted to hurt Billy by hurting Brandy.

Unacceptable, which was why he was leaving town tomorrow morning. A small vacation that the chief would be required to give, as he would claim mental trauma from seeing a person he'd just been talking to dead in a hail of bullets. She'd know it was bullshit, but she could hardly say no given the new emphasis on mental health in the workplace.

Billy didn't leave the precinct until late enough he should go right home and to bed. Instead, he swung by Brandy's place. He drove by. Didn't see a light, nor any out-of-place cars. Then again, how would he know? It wasn't as if he ran the plates of everyone to see if they had legitimate business in the area. Assuming that if Brunner and Koover had an accomplice they even knew where Brandy lived. He'd only found out because of Dorian. It wasn't as easy as people thought to legally access personal information on people who did a good job keeping their online traces private. Brandy's social media only said she lived in Ottawa. She was unlisted. If it weren't for his connections, he wouldn't have her address.

Meaning it was unlikely any possible accomplice of Koover or Brunner did either, else why not go after her at home? It was his guess they followed him and, when they saw his date, saw an opportunity to do harm.

Harm to Brandy.

He almost broke his steering wheel. He needed to make sure he didn't put her in danger again. While he saw no one following, he took no chances and didn't park anywhere close to her place. He chose to leave it a street over in a place where the light flickered, making visibility shit. Sticking to shadows, he took a looping route back to her place, keeping an eye out for any watchers. The hackles on his neck didn't stir at all, and so he took the stairs to her apartment two at a time.

The dark windows indicated she'd probably gone to bed, and yet, he had to be sure. Because what if Brunner and Koover had just been distractions? What if this *he* Brunner talked about acted without them? Never mind the fact Ulric most likely checked in on her and would have texted if something were amiss. Billy had to see her for himself.

Using some lockpicks with more ease than his police union would like, he let himself in quietly. Her apartment smelled of her and that damnable cat, which chose to greet him by climbing his leg until she could rub her head against the underside of his jaw.

He carried the kitten into the bedroom and saw the empty bed. He might have panicked if he'd not heard the front door suddenly open behind him. He didn't need to turn to know Brandy entered.

"Don't make any sudden moves or else."

"Or else what?" Billy asked as he turned to see her holding an umbrella menacingly.

"Billy? I wasn't expecting you. Next time some warning would be good. I almost whacked you." She waggled her umbrella at him before dropping it into a bucket by the door with two others.

"I came by to see how you were doing, but you weren't here." He couldn't help the hint of accusation.

"Because I was out."

"Why would you do that after what happened?" he barked, more aggressively than warranted. Blame the day he'd had.

"What happened was a fluke, and in case you hadn't noticed, I am a grown-ass woman capable of making my own decisions. Which, in this case, involved bandaging up Dorian. Some guy cut him off when he was riding his bike, and he ended up doing a header." She'd already shut the door, but now she locked it, as if assuming he'd stay. Given the cat currently sleeping against his chest, he might not have a choice.

"I'll never understand the bike thing," he muttered. The moment he could drive, he'd given up two wheels for four. Heck, he'd give up two legs for four more often, too, if he could.

"I thought about getting one to shorten my walking commute, but the thought of carting it up and down stairs each day…" Her nose wrinkled adorably.

It was irrational for him to want to offer to lug it for

her. He glanced away and cleared his throat. "So you don't have to worry about those guys who tried to abduct you last night."

"Why would I have worried? I had Detective Gruff on the job." She kicked off her ankle-high rubber boots and shrugged off her damp coat.

Her nonchalance bothered. "This isn't a joke. They're dead." He could have kicked himself when she went pale. While he couldn't hide the truth, not with the news carrying the story, he could have said it more gently.

"Wait, that shootout was with the guys who tried to kidnap me? What happened?"

"The case is a little complicated, and there are many unclear parts. Starting with why they went after you. But I wanted to reassure you that they're dead."

"Suicide by cop? Seems kind of drastic. Did they admit anything before taking themselves out?"

He flattened his lips. "No." He didn't mention the possibility of a third man. Now that he knew they were after him, once he removed himself from the equation, Brandy would be safe.

"I wonder if they were high," she mused aloud. "Then again, the fact they conspired to drug me and had a getaway car waiting in an alley shows a certain degree of planning."

"Doesn't matter anymore since they're dead."

"Which is also rather shocking. I need some wine." She padded to a small wine rack sitting on the floor and pulled out a bottle of red. She waggled it. "Join me in having a glass?"

"I really shouldn't. I just stopped by to check on you."

"People might notice if you leave too quickly, you know, given we're supposed to be a thing."

Now was the time to say it was over. That they wouldn't be seeing each other again for her safety—and not because she destroyed his peace of mind.

"Just one glass."

"Only one? I'm surprised that you, as a guy, would want to leave so quickly."

"Why?" he asked cautiously.

"Do you want a nickname like Two-Minute Wonder or Fast Draw McGruff?" She winked.

"It's wine— We're not—" he stammered.

"As a newly minted couple, people will expect we're doing it."

"No one saw me come in."

"That you know of," she countered.

More like he prayed because he'd never forgive himself if Brandy's association with him got her hurt. "You know what, I should go."

"Oh stop being so serious. Sit down. Relax." She thrust a glass of wine at him.

One wouldn't hurt. Neither would two. By three, he was actually relaxed and playing along with Brandy's game of three things people don't know about me.

Brandy sat sideways on the couch with her legs tucked under her. "So even Maeve doesn't know this, but I like to sing Justin Bieber songs in the shower."

He snickered. "I can see why you'd hide that."

"Is it my fault he makes great shower songs?" Her lips curved deliciously. "Your turn."

It took him a moment, mostly because the sharing of intimate details just wasn't something Billy ever did. Blame the alcohol for him blurting out, "I like watching romcoms."

"You?" She blinked. She recovered enough to ask, "What's your favorite?"

His cheeks heated as he admitted, "*The Princess Bride*."

"No way!" Brandy exclaimed. "I freaking love that movie." She then puffed out her chest and lowered her voice, "'My name is Inigo Montoya. You killed my father. Prepare to die.'" She held up her wine glass, and he tapped his against it, which led to her refilling it again.

"What other thing does no one know about you?" Billy asked.

She held out her hand. "When I make toast, I pretend I have Jedi powers that pop it up."

Her admission had him grinning. "I've done that with elevators."

Her laughter warmed him even more than the wine. "Maybe we're both secret Jedi heroes stuck on Earth for something special."

"As if you need help being any more awesome." The words slipped out, and he covered by taking a big chug of wine.

"Ah, Billy, you say the sweetest things, but you won't think I'm so great once I admit I am sometimes lazy about doing laundry and have been known to sniff test from the dirty pile."

Laughter burst from him as he exclaimed, "Me too!"

"Your turn. What other secrets do you have?"

He shrugged. "I'm a pretty basic guy."

"Says the werewolf." She rolled her eyes. "Like how did that come about? Was your dad one?"

"Fuck no." And a good thing, too, given his violent temper. "My parents were the lowest of trailer trash. Which is pretty fucking low, given there's so few year-around trailer parks in Ontario." His lips turned down. "I did the world a favor when I got snipped and made sure I wouldn't pass on their genes.

"I disagree. You're a good person."

He snorted. "Not really."

"You must be because Griffin chose you to be one of his Pack. From what I heard, he doesn't bite just anyone."

"I sometimes wonder if it was a pity bite, given the shit hand I got dealt."

"How does that happen anyhow? Like did he ask you first? Ulric says he knew about werewolves 'cause his dad was one for a pack up in North Bay."

"I knew Griffin and his family. They lived next door to my foster home." Which had since been sold. One of his foster moms died of uterine cancer a few years ago, and the other moved back to Europe to be with family.

"And?" She leaned forward eagerly. "How did it happen? Did he make you watch a bunch of werewolf movies to see if you were keen on it? Swear you to secrecy?"

"More like he got me really drunk. We drank an ungodly amount, although I realize now Griffin and the others were never as wasted as me because of their metabolism."

"Must be nice. I'm such a lightweight in comparison." She tipped her glass and her ruby-red wine-stained lips curved.

He wanted to suck the juice from them. Instead, he downed his glass and poured another. "Anyhow, once I was lit, we played a game that involved biting. Since we all had bite marks the next day, I thought nothing of it."

She stared, wide-eyed. "That's it? He bit you and then nothing?"

"Well, he waited to see what would happen."

"I can't believe he didn't say anything," she muttered.

"No point in telling me anything unless it worked."

"And what if it had? What if you'd changed spontaneously? Or gotten a woman pregnant? Ulric told me its deadly to the mother."

"I didn't change, and as to the whole impregnation thing, I was already snipped for a few years by then."

Her mouth snapped shut as she grasped he'd done it of his own volition. He'd never done it as a requisite for the Lycan change but to ensure he never did to a kid what his parents did to him.

"I thought doctors wouldn't do it to someone that young?"

"There's always an exception to the rule." It didn't take much to convince one when willing to pay cash for the procedure.

"So what was it like the first time you changed?" she asked, nursing her glass of wine.

His wine glow had begun to wear off. He really should leave. He poured another as he pondered a reply. "The first full moon after the bite, Griffin asked me to go camping with him and the boys." At the time, he'd been working as a constable for the Ottawa police and Griffin was a member of the Ottawa Pack, not an alpha. That came later. But the alpha of the time groomed Griffin to take over, and part of that included creating his own Lycans, people that would be loyal to him by blood and bite.

"Ooh, boys' wild weekend."

"Understatement. We went deep into the boonies. Like crazy deep, to the point I could hear banjos."

She laughed. "Oh my god. You watch horror movies."

"They're not as scary once you realize you are one of the monsters."

"Werewolves aren't monsters. Not in the books I read." She winked at him, and he had to look away.

Her allure only increased the more they spoke. But this was okay. He'd be leaving, and that would be the end of it. Might as well enjoy the little bit he had left.

"Lycans can be monsters, but on that night, we were simply men who could change into fur. It started by feeling itchy in my own skin." A fever burned within him, and his clothes irritated. "I remember Griffin kneeling in front of me and saying the pain would be fleeting." It was true, and yet at the time, the intense tearing had made him scream, only he had no voice as it happened. He changed rapidly and violently. Flesh to fur and howling at the end.

Griffin remained in front of him that entire time. Explaining.

"He told me that I was one of the chosen few. Special enough to handle the gift he'd given me." And to Billy, it had been a gift, that of acceptance and family. A family he'd then had to eschew to protect. Being a cop meant so much sacrifice.

"He was right about one thing; you are special. Howling-moon special." She winked as she threw her head back and uttered a husky croon.

"Smartass. Your turn now. How did you become the Brandy of today?"

"With boring-ass older parents. They had me in their forties. Dad went first of a heart attack. Mom of a bee sting of all things. She was an avid gardener. Maeve's all I've got left really that I'd call family."

"You know you can count on me and the Pack." For a guy who wanted nothing to do with her, he kept giving her a reason to call him back.

"To werewolf heroes!" She held out her glass, they clinked, and she chugged. She pointed to where he could find more wine, and he finally shook his head. "It's time for me to depart and for you to go to bed."

Her lips turned down. "Leaving already?"

He didn't want to. "It's late." And she was too drunk for him to tell her why he'd really come over.

"Bedtime!" she chirped. "Did you know there's a monster under mine? And the only way to avoid him is a solid leap."

It seemed only natural to say, "I'll walk you to bed so nothing can get you."

"My hero!" She clasped her hands and grinned as she swayed.

She weaved a little going to her bedroom. He wasn't too steady himself. The kitten didn't like that he swayed and leaped from his neck to the bed then the floor. He oddly missed the warm cuddly warmth.

He leaned forward and whipped back the blankets. "Your monster-free bed awaits."

"Why thank you, Detective." She crawled in and kept going to the far side before patting the space beside her. "Join me?"

"I can't. I gotta go." Because she looked utterly too tempting.

"You're in no condition to drive just yet."

She had a point.

"I'll stretch out on the couch." A couch that would be cramped.

She snorted. "Don't be silly. You'll wake up a wreck if you do that."

"Ulric did it."

"Ulric isn't my pretend boyfriend. Come on." She patted again. "I won't bite. Unless you want me to," she slyly added.

The word "bite" caused his gums to ache suddenly. Especially since his gaze veered to her neck. "I really should—"

Before he could finish, she'd leaned over and hauled at his hand, throwing him off balance. He landed on the mattress, the room spinning.

"Maybe I'll lie here for a few minutes." Once Brandy fell asleep, he'd sneak out before he did anything he shouldn't. Like kiss those wine stained lips.

He lay there stiffly. Not so Brandy. She curled against him, a warm and cuddly presence who murmured, "I'm glad you stopped by."

So was he. Wait, wasn't he supposed to be telling

her they'd never see each other again?

Later.

He relaxed slightly as the warmth of her permeated. Her breathing evened as she slipped into sleep. Moving too soon might wake her, so he waited, even as the wine and the exhaustion of the day caught up with him.

He fell asleep and dreamed of the woman by his side.

9

Brandy dreamt Billy was in her bed, wearing too many clothes. He looked positively delicious, his rugged jaw line teasing her to trace it with a finger. A finger that then went exploring, tugging up the hem of his shirt to skim over taut flesh.

Yes, he might sleep, and, no, he'd not exactly given her permission, but this was her dream. Her fantasy. And in it, he woke, his gaze meeting hers.

"Brandy." Her name emerged as a soft murmur.

"Shh." Speaking might ruin the moment. She leaned in for a kiss, pressing her mouth to his softly, gently at first. But it soon turned passionate, their mouths devouring and meshing in a fiery embrace. She rolled atop him, reveling in how real it felt.

"We shouldn't," he muttered, even as he sucked her lower lip.

"Why not?" She wiggled atop him, annoyed by the amount of clothes separating them.

She began tugging at his hem, pulling his shirt upward. "Why are you dressed in my dream?" she grumbled.

He grabbed at her hands. "This isn't a dream. And we have to stop. You had a bit too much wine. We both did."

"This isn't because of the wine." How to make him understand the euphoria she was under had nothing to do with alcohol and everything with desire? "I want you."

"I'm sorry. I can't." He looked and sounded pained by the words.

She ached, too, but for a different reason.

"If you're not going to play, then you can watch." She rolled onto her back and shimmied out of her pants and her panties before she spread her legs and slid a hand between her thighs.

"Brandy." He moaned her name.

Her reply involved slipping her fingers into her slit to get them damp before rubbing them over her nub. She felt no shame despite the fact he watched. On the contrary, having him as her audience only increased her need.

"You're killing me," he groaned.

Yet he didn't leave her bed.

"Then join in. And before you say you can't"—she eyed his groin—"your hard-on says otherwise."

"You're still tipsy from the wine."

"Not really." She glowed, but that was more from arousal than any lingering effect of the alcohol. She kept touching herself, rubbing faster.

When he shifted on the bed, it wasn't to leave it but to slide between her legs, his face pushing her thighs apart. Her fingers might have felt nice stroking her clit, but the flick of his tongue had her hips arching.

He grabbed hold of her and held her still, a prisoner to his pleasuring. A willing prisoner.

She arched as he flicked his tongue. Cried out when he slid a finger into her. Came hard, bucking and panting.

Only then did he climb up her body for a kiss, letting her taste herself on his lips. She wrapped her arms around him, even as he murmured, "I should go."

"Stay. I'm not done yet." She once more tugged at his shirt. This time he helped her remove it, leaving him bare-chested, his pants low on his hips. She reached for the waistband, and he put a hand over her greedy fingers.

"Are you sure?"

"You're really taking this consent thing too far. Yes, I'm sure. Are you?" she asked, staring him in the eyes.

He said nothing for a moment. His thumb brushed over her lower lip. "Do you know how many times I've dreamed of this moment? Even now, I wonder if this is real."

She reached inside his pants and grabbed him, squeezing him tight enough he gasped.

"This is happening. I think we've both danced around it long enough." She unbuttoned and unzippered his pants enough to free his hard cock. Her hand wrapped around it and tugged. His hips followed as he braced himself on his forearms above her.

"Kiss me," she demanded as she finally released his cock, knowing she wouldn't be able to hold on.

"If you insist." He leaned down and took her mouth passionately, the hard slant of his lips setting her aflame. Her legs were spread wide to accommodate his body. It didn't take much angling and thrusting of her hips to convince the tip of his cock to poke her in the right spot.

He groaned as he slid deeper into her, taking his sweet bloody time. She nipped his lip and growled, "Stop being so damned gentle. I won't break." And she'd scream if he took it any slower.

With a strangled moan, he thrust into her. The long tip of him butted her in the G-spot, giving her that jolt of pleasure that hitched her breath.

He stretched her perfectly, tapped her right on the money each time. His pace got faster the harder she clutched at him. Faster. Head tilted back, she panted. Harder. She keened as her nails dug in deeper to his biceps as she held on to the wild ride.

"Look at me." His growled command had her locking gazes with him. The depths of his orbs glowed, even as she saw herself reflected in them. Passion-flushed, wild, untamed.

His.

"Billy." She sighed his name as she felt herself coming. A slow, roiling wave of pleasure that had her mouth opening wide with no sound. Her nails dug deep. Her entire body clenched as she sat on the edge of orgasm, every single muscle seized. She even stopped breathing.

Her eyes remained locked with his. His hips ground against her, just rubbing the tip, over and over, deep, so deep. She threw back her head, and her back arched as her orgasm hit. Billy cradled her to his chest. Cuddling her as pleasure pulsed through her body. She sucked at his flesh, as she squeezed his cock tight. Felt the heat as he came.

She rolled into another orgasm before the first one was even done. Rather than scream, she sank her teeth into him. Hard. Firmly. Definitely bruising, probably breaking skin, and yet she couldn't ease the pressure with the pleasure pumping through her.

He uttered a sharp cry, and then she felt the sting of his bite, followed by a strange heat that prolonged her pulsing climax.

By the time their passion was spent, they collapsed in a pile of limbs. Mostly naked. He still had his pants on up to the swell of his ass.

Given he cradled her and had his head tucked over hers, she could grope those cheeks and revel in that she'd finally gotten to shag the real and not dream version of Billy. He was even better than she'd imagined.

He muttered, "What have we done?"

"The naughty. Although, next time, even though I am on the pill, we should use a condom."

He stared at her. "I can't get you pregnant."

"I know that, but what about an STD?" she retorted as Billy predictably ruined the moment.

"I'm no— That is—" he blustered. "I have to go."

He practically fell out of the bed in his haste. He yanked up his pants, dove at his shirt, which had landed on a chair, and raced out of her bedroom so damned fast she was almost insulted.

But she gave him a pass due to his suffering from shock. She had a bit of it herself.

Once the door slammed shut, she rose and went to the bathroom to see the proof herself.

A bite mark on her boob. From all the romance books she'd read, she knew what that meant.

I'm his mate.

10

SHE'S NOT MY MATE.

She couldn't be, and yet he'd seen the mark on her breast. A crescent moon bite he'd not meant to do and yet, in the moment, in the epic pleasurable moment, he couldn't help himself.

It meant nothing. Never mind supposed Lycan lore about fate and finding "the one." Never settling down. That was what he'd promised himself. Because relationships always started out well, on a high from love, and then went downhill from there. Look at his parents.

What about everyone else? his subconscious argued, not for the first time. It liked to point out his toxic parents weren't exactly a model example.

Didn't matter in any case. Brandy wasn't his mate. He'd just been caught up in the moment. And besides, the bite thing was a Hollywood myth. He was pretty sure Griffin hadn't bitten Maeve. Then again, he'd never asked.

No. It means nothing.

He kept repeating that to himself as he walked rapidly to his car parked a block away. He found it untouched. The hour was later than expected, only an hour until dawn. They must have slept longer than he realized, meaning he couldn't even blame the alcohol for his actions. He'd lost control because it was Brandy.

A woman who terrified him more than any criminal he'd run down.

The apartment building across from his townhouse had some windows showing light. Lots of workers with early starts. The outside parking had a few cars idling, started via remote. He parked in his driveway, not the garage, which was reserved for his bike. He entered through the front door of his place, tossing his keys on the table even as he nudged the portal shut.

He didn't stop his usual routine, even as he sensed the wrongness in his place. The darkness was more intense than usual, as if someone had drawn the blinds. He flicked a light switch in the entrance, illuminating the space.

A place utterly destroyed.

"What the ever-loving fuck," he huffed as he took in the damage. Nothing remained intact, from the pictures torn from the wall, the canvas ripped, to the stuffing yanked from the cushions on his couch. In the kitchen, the fridge had been toppled and food was everywhere.

His bedroom held a message on the wall above the massacred bed: *I'm coming for you.*

It seemed his problems hadn't ended with the death of Brunner and Koover.

With nothing in his place to salvage, he exited. On his way back to his car, he called Ulric since he wasn't about to bother Griffin on his honeymoon.

"Whatever it is, Detective, I didn't do it," Ulric answered.

"Someone trashed my place last night." He didn't mean to blurt it out.

"Fuck dude, that sucks. Any idea who it is?"

"I think it's related to those guys who pulled suicide by cop at the station. I arrested both of them in the past. It's got to be some sort of vendetta, and if the other night proved anything, it's that those close to me aren't safe."

"Ah, were you worried about me, Gruff?"

"More like worried about Brandy. My apartment was trashed by someone other than Brunner and Koover meaning there's still someone out there with a grudge."

"Need help hunting them down?"

"I can handle that part. What I need is Brandy to be safe, seeing as how our recent charade brought her into the crosshairs." The word "charade" brought a bad taste to his mouth because it hadn't felt fake. Their connection, even apart from the sex, had been all too real and epic. Also memorable? The way he'd leaped out of that bed and fled that apartment. No apology. No explanation. Nothing.

He cleared his throat as he lost his train of thought and restarted. "Because I've been pretending to date Brandy, she might be a target too."

"Are you still at her place?"

"Um…" He didn't know what he should admit.

"Dude, I am aware you guys are an item. I texted her last night."

"Why?" He didn't mean to bark it.

"Calm down. I was gonna come over to kick her ass at virtual bowling, only she messaged back that she had her boyfriend over."

"She called me her boyfriend?" He diluted his pleasure by the reminder she'd found a way to text last night without him knowing it. Probably when he went to pee.

"Yes, she called you boyfriend. Are you going to giggle like a schoolgirl about it?"

"Fuck off."

"Does this mean I won our bet?"

"No, because we didn't place a bet. And I didn't call to fuck around. I need you to head over to Brandy's right now."

"Can't, dude. Not for a little bit anyhow."

"But she needs protection now."

"Hold on, you left her alone knowing there was still a psycho on the loose?"

"At the time, I didn't know. And in my weak defense, the two guys who tried to kidnap her are dead. But given the trashed appearance of my apartment, there is at least one or more left."

"Holy fuck, how many people did you piss off?" Ulric sounded impressed.

"Plenty, which is why I don't want Brandy left alone. At least until we know I've drawn them away from her."

"While I understand your need and want to help, I still can't get over there for at least an hour. And then what am I supposed to tell her? Hey, Billy wants me to hang out until he calls the all clear?"

The very idea of Ulric staying with her had him seething. Billy shoved it down. "Actually, I don't think Brandy should stay at her apartment. Think Griffin and Maeve would mind if she stayed at their place over the shop for the next little bit?" It had excellent security.

"That's not a bad idea. Me and Quinn and Dorian can take turns in the bunker." A fancy name for a room outfitted with a bed, three-piece bathroom, and a weapons locker in case they really needed to defend the shop and the pack.

"Appreciate it. I'll let you know when it's safe again."

"What's the plan?"

"Going to draw him away from the city and take him out."

"Him? Kind of sexist, bro."

"Not really. Before he died, Brunner claimed he took orders from another man. I don't have the impression it was Koover, since he died, too." Not to mention, he was dumb as rocks.

"So you're using yourself as bait. Who's your backup closing the trap?" Ulric asked.

"No one. I can handle it."

"Said many dead men."

"I'll be at the cabin where I have complete advantage."

"And isolation. Once you're there, you're cut off from the outside world. You won't be able to call for help."

"It's the perfect place to quietly dispose of a problem."

"What if it's not just one guy?" Ulric pointed out. "What if they bring guns? It's more than two weeks until the next full moon."

Closer to three. Billy could feel its approach. "You forget that I'm a crack shot." As soon as Billy learned how to use a gun, he'd honed his target practice skills.

"We should talk to Griffin."

"No. The man is on his honeymoon. It will be fine."

"Famous last words," Ulric grumbled. "So when do you leave?"

"Apparently right after you get to Brandy's place."

Because he couldn't leave her without a guard. The problem was if he parked out front, he might as well announce her location and his interest. But at the same time, being parked blocks away wouldn't do any damned good.

Once more, he parked elsewhere and walked to her place, snaring coffee and donuts on his path given the early hour. What he would have to say would need sugar and caffeine.

Hat pulled low, shoulders hunched to disguise his true shape, he knocked on her door. The moment it opened, he muttered a grim, "We need to talk."

Brandy, wearing only a flimsy silk robe, arched her brow. "Do we? Because I'm not sure if I should talk to a guy who not only couldn't stick around a few minutes to cuddle but ran out the door without even saying goodbye."

He winced. "It was bad of me. And there is no defense for my actions. I'm sorry." He held out his treats. "I brought food and caffeine."

"Bring it in." She stepped aside, and he entered, cautiously.

She appeared angry and calm at the same time.

Before he could make it to the kitchen, the cat came out of nowhere, leaped, hit his pant leg, and climbed.

"What the fuck!" he yelped as those sharp, tiny daggers called claws dug into his poor flesh.

"Don't yell. You'll scare her, and then it's worse," Brandy advised as she perched on a stool at her breakfast bar. A glorified word for the tiny bit of counter overlooking the living room.

The kitten made it to his waist and meowed. He cupped it and brought it to his shoulder, where it settled, purring raggedly against his ear. Billy set down the bag of treats and tray of coffees. He pointed. "There's extra cream and sugar just in case I got it wrong."

"I'm more interested in the donuts you grabbed. You can tell a lot about a person by the donuts they chose. Cruller? Soft and sweet. Chocolate, full of energy. Plain? Psychopath, stay away. And if you see a sign of a bran muffin? *Run.*" She winked as she rummaged, pulling them out one by one.

Maple cream, blueberry Danish, sprinkle-covered, honey glazed, chocolate glazed, and sourdough.

"Not bad," she murmured before choosing the Danish. She peeled the lid from her coffee and dipped it. "Mmm."

He just stared at her mouth. A mouth that he'd kissed. The taste of her lingered. His desire for her remained unabated, given his sudden erection. His hands dropped to cover the bulge, as if she wouldn't know the reason.

Brandy waved her half-eaten Danish at him. "Aren't you having some?"

"I'm not hungry. I'm here to apologize for taking advantage of you last night."

A snort crinkled her nose. "That's funny. If anyone took advantage, it was me. You were just so delicious looking. I had to have me some Billy Gruff." She winked.

He fought not to sputter. "It can never happen again."

"Well, that seems kind of a cruel thing to say, given those were some of the best orgasms I've ever had. Like talk about intense."

His cheeks turned a ruddy color. "Uh..."

"Why, Detective, are you blushing?"

"No." The praise pleased, and his resolve wavered. He only had to remember his apartment and the dead men to bolster his determination. "Listen, last night was fun, but right now just isn't a good time. I've got these guys after me because of some vendetta, and apparently that's why they went after you."

"Those guys are dead."

"There's still another one. They trashed my place, and they might come after you next, which is why you need to go stay somewhere else for a little bit."

"Excuse me?" She blinked.

"Just for a while until I handle the threat."

"Oh, *you* will." She took a sip of her coffee. "Isn't that misogynistic of you."

"How is keeping you safe sexist?"

"Because I can take care of myself."

"The fuckers who tried to kidnap you brought guns into a police station. The one that's still alive annihilated my apartment. This is serious."

"Then let me help. After all, we're mates."

"Er, what?" His turn to flutter his lashes in confusion.

"You know, mated. I'm wearing your mark." She tugged her robe to the side to show him the crescent-shaped bite.

Oh, fuck.

"About that…I shouldn't have done that. Only you chomped me, and I kind of lost my head."

"And your load. Totally normal." She offered a sage nod.

"Again, sorry. It won't happen again."

"Of course not. Any future nibbling will be the erotic kind. The claiming only happens the first time, according to the books I've read."

He ogled her. "What books?"

"Don't laugh, but when I couldn't find out much about the whole werewolf thing, I went reading. Only there doesn't seem to be much outside romance stories."

"You read romance books about werewolves?" His jaw might never get off the floor.

"Mostly. Some had shapeshifters, you know folks who can turn into something else. I will say, according to these authors, having only men capable of the change is extremely rare. Are you sure it's not doable for women?"

He nodded.

"Pity. I wouldn't have minded giving it a go. But at least you'll be comforted knowing I am accepting of your other half."

"No. No you're not." He backed away. "You. Me. We're not a thing."

"The bite mark says otherwise."

"It means nothing. It was an accident."

"Which I'm sure you're man enough to take responsibility for. After all, I am not making excuses. I fully admit I wanted to bite you."

"You were drunk."

"Not by the time we started making out."

"You were half asleep," he hastened to point out in desperation. "You thought it was a dream at first."

"Tell you what, I'm wide awake right now. Want to bet you'll be wearing my teeth again by the time we're done?" she purred.

Whelp.

Could she hear the terror—and aching desire—to let her do just that?

She snared a cream-filled donut, and he couldn't help but stare as she licked her lips after each bite.

He cleared his throat. "Once Ulric gets here, I'm leaving to deal with the threat."

"Ah yes, off to find your nemesis. Once you get

back, dinner at my place? I'll provide the wine and dessert."

"I won't be back. I was wrong to get involved in the first place," he admitted.

"I knew you'd say that. So predictable, Billy Gruff. You want me, yet you're afraid of me."

"I'm not afraid."

"Says the man who ran away from intimacy."

"I told you I don't do relationships."

"Because you hadn't yet met me."

"You're not listening."

"You're right, I'm not, because if there's one thing I know, Billy Gruff, it's that you and I are meant to be together." She advanced on him, and he backed away until he hit a wall.

He swallowed hard. "Why would you want me of all people? I can't give you kids, or even a promise of safety. I have enemies."

"That you don't have to fight alone. As for kids... We can always get more cats." The one at his neck growled as if in disagreement.

He changed tactics. "I'm a cop. Everyone hates cops."

"Always did love me a man in uniform."

He uttered a very unmanly sound as she destroyed all his arguments and chiseled at his resolve. "I have to go," he grumbled.

"Where? I thought you said your apartment was trashed."

"I have a place. Far from here."

"Then I guess I'd better get my kiss goodbye while I can." She lunged for him suddenly and grabbed him by the shirt. Dragged him close. Her mouth pressed hotly against his, and he was weak.

That flimsy robe didn't stand a chance. It parted at his touch, and with her naked underneath, it was too easy to lift her and slide into her. His fingers dug into her cheeks as he bounced her. Her lips locked to his, panting and wet.

So wet.

She slid perfectly up and down on him. Slick. Tight.

Mine.

They came together in an orgasm that left his legs trembling. He barely made it to the couch to deposit her. He righted his clothes as she lay sprawled and smiling.

"Hmm. With that kind of goodbye, I can't wait until you come back for my hello."

"Did you not hear what I said before?"

"You think you can walk away. You can try, but I guarantee you and I aren't done, Billy Gruff."

Why did her threat have to sound so sweet?"

"Lock the door," was the last thing he said as he fled her apartment. He practically flew down the stairs when he bolted.

But did he leave right away? Nope. He skulked the neighborhood and waited for Ulric to arrive.

Only then did he leave and start the task of catching a tail. If he wanted whoever it was to come after him, then they needed to follow. Billy went back to this apartment. Then popped in to his work. Even stopped at his favorite grocery store.

He didn't see a shadow, but it didn't matter. He'd left a visible trail. If someone was looking for Billy, they'd find him.

11

Billy literally bolted as if he did indeed have Canadian geese chasing after him. Kind of ballsy given his whole spiel. *It was an accident. I don't want to date.* And then the crowning excuse: *Bad guys are after me, so I'm gonna leave to protect you.*

Dick.

Brandy ate another donut. When the door—which she'd not yet gotten her lazy ass up to lock—swung open, she expected to see Billy. Because, hello, as her mate—and according to countless romance books—he shouldn't be able to resist her.

Instead of a sexy detective, she got Ulric.

"Oh, it's you."

His eyebrow arched as he drawled, "Wow, way to stroke my ego."

"As if any part of you needs stroking." She wrinkled her nose. "Why are you here?"

"Didn't Billy tell you?"

"Billy said a lot of things." Most of them dumb. Like him.

"Pack your stuff and get ready for an exciting staycation at Chez Lanark."

"I am not going anywhere." She stuck her feet up on the table. Crossed her arms. Did every childish maneuver she could think of.

"Gonna throw yourself on the floor and pound it while screaming if I say too bad?"

"Maybe. I just don't see why I have to leave my apartment. The two guys who came after me are dead."

"There's still someone else out there."

"So Billy claimed. And then he left. Tells me I'm in danger. Because of him. And then out the door he goes."

Ulric winced. "I agree his decision was kind of odd. But that's Billy. He looks at things differently on account he's a cop."

"A cop who left to make himself bait." Brandy swung her feet off the table and leaned forward, huffing, "I can't believe he actually left."

"If it's any consolation, the place he's going is very familiar to him. He'll have the upper hand there."

"Or paw. Maybe he'll be able to shift without the moon again."

Ulric offered a non-committal, "Maybe."

"Does he often run away?" she asked boldly.

"Actually, this is a first. Guess you scared him good with the relationship thing."

Had she come on too strong? Too bad. She wasn't about to lie about what she wanted. "What if this enemy he's created never appears? How long will he stay in hiding?"

"He can probably do an easy week or two before his work gets antsy. He's worked hard on his career. I can't see him tanking it."

Two weeks. Surely she could wait that long. Give him his space. Then confront him.

"What's he so hung up about? And don't tell me his parents. Surely a smart guy like him knows they're not indicative of most relationships."

Ulric snorted. "You'd be surprised. Do you know what age he had his vasectomy?"

"He said young and before he knew anything about Lycans."

"The guy had himself sterilized at twenty-one. I'd say whatever he experienced with his parents, they traumatized him good." Ulric's soft claim had her chewing her lower lip.

"But how will he ever learn differently if he can't make it past a few dates?"

"Few?" Ulric whistled. "In college, Billy was known as the one-night-stand man. He never slept with the same woman twice."

"So he was a whore."

"Actually, he was picky about who he slept with,

which was the reason why he probably got away with it. When he started looking, the pussies threw themselves at him."

She wrinkled her nose. "TMI!"

"If you're going to pick my brain about Billy, you're going to get it from the perspective of a male that partied at college. Took me an extra year to get a degree I never actually used."

"What did you study?" she asked.

"Criminology, same as Billy. Only he actually got a job with his. Now, if we're done with the Billy hour, get your butt into gear and pack a bag. The game starts at one, which only gives us a few hours to prep all the snacks we'll need."

The idea of gorging on appetizers—nachos, queso, wings, deviled eggs, pickles, mini bagel pizzas, potato skins, caramel popcorn—had her almost salivating. And Griffin's television spanned an epic one hundred inches because he used a projector and a drop-down screen.

But then she'd be doing what Billy wanted. A man who had no problem walking—very quickly—away.

"And what of Froufrou? She can't stay in the loft. Way too many places for her to escape or get stuck." Kittens were cute, but dumb.

"Um, I guess she can stay with me." Ulric eyed her baby currently curled in a ball in the tiny ring of sunlight hitting the floor.

"You'll need to pack her things. Litter box, food bowl, water bowl, snack bowl." She ticked off her fingers. "Then you'll need the dry food in the pink container, the yellow, and if this is going to last more than three days, also the blue. Plus cans from the cupboard."

Ulric staggered to his feet and began hunting for stuff. Brandy went into her room and got changed then packed a bag, all comfortable stuff. Plus toiletries, plus snacks, the good ones, which she kept in her nightstand. As she gathered stuff for a few days' stay, she kept thinking she forgot something.

She wasn't alone. She emerged to find Ulric eyeing a tower of cat supplies on the floor. "I feel like I am missing something," the big man muttered.

"Better hope not. Froufrou can be particular." Her kitten purred as she weaved and rubbed between her ankles. Seemingly happy. She'd mostly likely pounce the moment Brandy moved.

"I'll need a bin to carry it."

"I have reusable fabric bags under the kitchen sink."

She thought he would cry when he pulled them out and saw the size. Manageable for someone Brandy's size.

It took him a few trips, as he had to fill, dump, and return to refill and dump again. Then he had to carry her bag as she coaxed Froufrou into her very expensive carrying case, a large, sleek, gold-colored condo with a heated pad on the inside, a soothing scent, and a dulling of noise to relax felines.

Froufrou hated the eight-hundred-dollar prison. She hissed at Brandy.

"Come on, baby. It's just for a short ride." Ulric came in as she crooned, "I'll give you a fish stick, undercooked and smelly, for dinner."

"Can't you just grab her and stuff her in?"

"Do you like the use of your hands?" she asked quite frankly.

He gaped.

"I thought so," she muttered and held out her hand. "We have to go for a car ride. You'll be staying with Uncle Ulric."

"You know, you could too. I've got the pullout," he offered.

"No thanks. I will stick to a house that doesn't smell like pizza and man sweat."

"It's my home gym. I wipe it down each time."

"I'll stick with luxury, thank you. But will visit, so let's make sure there's no women's underwear sticking to the couch or floor."

"I'm thinking my apartment is connected to the dryer verse. Because how else is the underwear getting there?"

"Your dates."

"Surely they aren't leaving without them. Why would anyone leave their underpants behind?"

"Why do dogs pee on things?"

His mouth rounded. "Oh. Fuck. It seems kind of obvious now."

"Question for you. Why are you babysitting me instead of helping Billy? If someone is trying to hurt him, then isn't he the one in need of protection?"

"Billy's a stubborn son of a bitch."

"You don't say."

"And who says he's not protected?"

She pursed her lips. "Who went with him?"

"No one. He's being shadowed."

"By who? Quinn?"

"No, Quinn is part of the rotation watching over you."

"What rotation? I only even found out you were making me leave my place like thirty minutes ago," she hotly exclaimed.

"Planning is a strong suit of mine." Ulric knelt and held out a hand. He puckered his lips to expel kissing noises.

Brandy might have mocked him, except Froufrou came sauntering out, tiny kitten belly swaying. She head-butted his hand before sitting in it. Ulric stood slowly with her cradled in his hand and tucked her close to his chest.

Froufrou remained only a moment before climbing up to nestle between his shoulder and neck. Ulric offered a side-eye to the cat. "Well, at least now we can leave."

"You can't go outside with her like that. What if she bolts?"

He grimaced. "Don't have a leash?"

"Put her in the condo," Brandy suggested sweetly.

"I thought she hated it."

"But she likes you."

"She does." Ulric beamed. "Come on, little kitty, let's get you— Argh!"

What followed next was the downfall of a giant, as a tiny kitten led Ulric on a chase that saw him getting almost as many stripes as a tiger.

Ulric sucked his bloody knuckles and fingers as he eyed Froufrou sitting and delicately licking a paw. "I think we need a new plan."

The moment he said it, the kitten chose to walk into the travel condo, curl up in a ball, and go to sleep.

She stayed that way the entire ride to Ulric's place, where he blushed as Brandy pointed to the panties on the ceiling fan.

"I swear those weren't there when I left." While he fetched the cat supplies from the car, Brandy did a circuit, looking for dangerous things for a kitten. There were no holes allowing access outside. Windows were all closed, and even if open, they possessed screens. The spare bedroom with its computer desk and gaming chair had plenty of room for the kitty litter box. The food went in the kitchen. When the cat condo door opened, Froufrou sauntered out then took off, whipping around the apartment, checking it out. Brandy waited until Froufrou settled down, choosing to sleep atop the fridge, before she left with Ulric for Maeve's new place with its open ceiling design with holes too tempting for a kitten to ignore.

As they drove over, she found herself asking, "Would you rather be with Billy?"

"He asked me to take care of you.

"I can take care of myself," she muttered.

"Like you did the other night?"

Her cheeks heated. "I didn't realize a stranger sent me that drink, or I would have never drunk it."

"Don't act like it's such a prison sentence. It will be fun. We'll order in food. Watch dumb movies."

"While Billy's off acting as tasty bait."

"Is he tasty?" Ulric teased.

"The finest I've ever had." And since Ulric was her friend, she dragged down her shirt and flashed him the upper part of her boob. "Look at this."

To his credit, he hissed and turned away. "What the fuck, Brandy?"

"Oh, calm down. I'm not showing any nipple. Check it out and tell me what it means."

Ulric turned to eye her, his gaze narrowing quickly on the bite mark. "Billy did that?"

She nodded.

"Well, damn. I didn't peg him for a wild kind of guy in the sack."

"It is what I think it is though, right?"

"It's a bite mark."

"Also known as a mating bite or a claiming mark. What word do you use for Lycan who chomps to identify his mate?"

Ulric blinked at her. "What are you yapping about? There's no such thing as a biting whatever the fuck you're calling it."

"Really? Oh." She couldn't help but sound deflated. "Guess that means he won't be mystically called back to my side because he can't handle being away from me."

"Oh, he'll be back. The very fact he ran from you instead of using you as bait tells us everything we need to know." Ulric paused for effect. "Billy's in love."

Brandy would have liked to believe it, only it became hard when, after three days, no one would admit to having heard from him. Never mind the fact he'd gone away for a reason. He didn't once try to contact her. He'd bedded and ghosted.

It led to some pity ice cream and much pacing. Massive windows brought in plenty of light. The kitchen boasted all the bells and whistles she needed to make herself epic feasts.

She stuck to Mickey D's, the bakery that delivered cakes, and pizza. The ice cream was the only thing that she couldn't order in. Ulric kept her stocked.

As she sucked the spoon, it occurred to her this was the first night since Billy walked out on her that she'd been alone. Ulric had to leave, as his aunt required him to drive her to weekly bridge. Quinn was late because of an accident on the highway. The cops were trying to reroute those caught in it. She'd promised to keep the doors locked and stay away from windows. So dumb. Nothing was going to happen. Three days and nothing untoward had happened at all.

Plink.

The noise startled her enough she stopped shoveling creamy, sugary goodness into her mouth. She glanced in the direction of the window. Not that she could see it, given the massive screen blocked a large section.

Tock.

Another knock sounded on the glass.

Probably just a bird. Definitely nothing to be scared of. To prove it to herself, she marched to the screen and then behind it to glance out the window. The road in front of the building showed a lone car moving in its lane, the streetlight illuminating an empty sidewalk, the shop—

Bang.

She startled as something slammed into the window where she'd been peeking.

A bird?

Wait, was that a bat?

It didn't come alone. As if drawn by the gaping astonishment shining from her face, a flock of winged creatures began to hit the glass hard enough it creaked. It didn't splinter, but Brandy backed away because it would take only one crack to shatter the whole pane.

Slipping to the other side of the screen out of sight didn't stop the barrage. Worse, it spread to the other windows. She suddenly remembered a movie her grandma used to watch with the tubby fellow, Hitchcock. A name that used to make her giggle. In it, birds attacked people for no apparent reason, killing them! She could only imagine bats would be worse.

Plink. Thunk. Crack.

Screw Ulric's orders. She wasn't staying in the apartment.

She snared a bag of chips and water, along with a blanket, as she went through the new security door at the top of the stairs. Another door at the bottom opened into the back room, which adjoined the employees' lounge and the tiny bunker. She burst into the space to see Quinn hadn't arrived yet.

No one sat at the desk with the computer. Or playing cards at the table set with four chairs. The coffee pot hadn't even been turned on.

Thump. The sound came from the door onto the alley.

She glanced at the security monitors mounted above the computer desk. The one above the alley exit showed no one there. Then a swooping dark shape slammed into the portal. It didn't recover and hit the ground, trembling only a moment before going still. Its failure didn't stop others from trying to bash their way in.

Why were they acting so strange?

The silence, when it fell, happened so suddenly it jarred. She stood there, unbreathing and listening.

The thumping had stopped. No more bats swooped on the monitors. However, a shadow did form on the screen overlooking the alley. A shadow so deep and dark the camera recording it died. The screen filled with a staticky jumble of gray, white, and black snow.

Ominous shit, which was why she texted Ulric. *Think I'm under attack.*

His aunt might need a ride, but he still had her back. *I need you to hold on for ten.*

She'd try, but her odds would really depend on what happened next.

The camera at the front of the store showed someone approaching, wearing a long trench, features covered in a mask, toting a chain saw.

Not good.

She closed her eyes and opened them again. Still a chainsaw and whoever it was yanked on its cord to start it.

Vroom. Vroom. He revved it as he approached the front of the shop.

She texted Ulric again. *Any suggestions on how to stop a chainsaw?*

Whing. Whing. The machine whirred and whined as it bit into the bars protecting the windows of the pot shop.

Hide. I'm a few minutes away.

Hide where?

She glanced around and saw nowhere that would hide her for long against a chain saw. Even the so-called bunker only had a regular door on it.

Crash. Glass shattered as the chain saw wielder cleared a spot big enough to kick in.

Any second now, she'd have company. She had to do something.

Anything.

Griffin didn't have any guns lying around. A shocking lack for a pot shop if you asked her. Since she knew the computer monitor would require her getting close, she instead grabbed one of the chairs from around the table. She hurried with it to the front and swung it as the person ducked to get through the hole they'd made in the window.

Wham. The guy staggered. Before she could think twice, she swung and connected again. But the fucker still didn't go down!

Worse, he smiled. "There you are. Come to me." He lunged.

She squeaked and swung. It didn't deter the man, who immediately came after her.

It took quite a few flings of the chair before the guy hit the edge of the counter and fell to the floor. He didn't get up.

Brandy heaved for breath. Panting. Terrified. A death grip on the chair just in case he twitched.

Ulric arrived first, slamming through the alley door,

racing in to see her standing over a body. "Brandy, are you okay?"

"Me, yes. Him, no. I think he's dead." She'd seen death before. Couldn't avoid it in a hospital. But this was the first one she'd actively caused. "I hit him with a chair."

"That wouldn't have killed him."

"I hit him several times, and he slammed into the counter hard when he went down." Her lips trembled. She was a murderer.

Did Ulric console her? Nope. The man scowled at the body, hands on his hips. "This is unfortunate. Dead men can't talk."

"What else was I supposed to do? He had a chainsaw!" Brandy pointed out the window to the thing on the sidewalk that looked more like a swordfish in repose.

Ulric wandered for a look. "That's actually a Sawzall, not a chainsaw. Great tool. Cuts through just about anything."

"I'm less interested in his toys than I am his motive. Do you think this is the guy that Billy was worried about?"

"Won't know for sure until we run his prints and find out who he is."

"And how long will that take? Billy should be told."

"I will the next time he checks in."

Brandy pursed her lips at the reminder that he'd

been in contact part of the time. Just not with her. "Surely there's an easier way to contact him."

"Short of driving out there?" Ulric shook his head.

"I could drive."

"Don't you even start." Ulric wagged his finger at her. "You're not supposed to go anywhere until we know the coast is clear."

She waved to the floor. "Cleared it."

"Maybe. What if Sawzall man is not connected to the Billy situation?"

"Really? Come on, that'd be a hell of a coincidence if he wasn't since he appeared to be looking for me."

"Was he? Or did you just happen to be in a pot shop when he broke in for his fix?"

"He said hey, there you are, which indicates he was looking for me and even if he wasn't, would you stop working against me? I'm trying to bring Billy home." Because she missed him something fierce.

"I will tell him the next time he checks in."

"Or I could surprise him in person." She offered a winsome smile.

It took an hour of her barraging Ulric before he finally caved and gave her the directions to where Billy was hiding—and a shadow named Dorian who followed her most of the way.

Ready or not, Billy Gruff, here I come.

12

Leaving the city was a cowardly thing to do. Billy could at least admit that to himself, even as he didn't like what that said about him. Still, what choice did he have?

Between the threat to him and the risk with Brandy, he'd never been more conflicted.

He couldn't be mated. He'd made a vow he would never, ever, become his parents.

Which led to his conscience whispering, *You're nothing like them.* For one, he didn't have a drinking problem like his dad. Two, he'd never hit a woman or a child. However, he did have the capability of violence. It was in his blood even before it became an accepted part of his Lycan nature.

I can kill. Directly or by device. He'd done it as man and beast. A beast more savage than Brandy understood.

She read these fantasy stories and imagined he was some kind of romantic hero with fur. The reality? The wolf pulsed inside his breast at the most inopportune time, pushing to get out. And when it did escape? It wanted to hunt. It didn't feel anything but satisfaction when it caused pain.

Friendship didn't count either. He'd wanted to eviscerate Ulric just for talking to Brandy. Being with her would only make that insanity worse. He still remembered his father's jealous rages. Completely unhinged to everyone but the man screaming, "*Whore!*"

Brandy deserved a normal relationship with a man carrying less baggage. Not to mention she shouldn't come to harm because some asshole wanted to settle a score with the cop that arrested his ass.

If you've got a beef, then bring it to me.

Which was why, when he fled, he left the biggest trail he could manage, sending out messages and texts. Speaking of it in every store and restaurant he hit on his way. "*Staying at my cabin at the end of Harvey's Road.*" An odd name, especially given research of the half-dozen addresses for it showed no previous or current landowner called Harvey.

His cabin resided a few hours from the city, bought years ago as a place he could use to be himself, so remote that his friends could meet him here and no one was the wiser about his relationship with the Pack. Off the grid with a generator for the times solar wasn't enough. A septic because he wasn't an animal. And running water, including hot, using a propane tank, the source being the well he had dug.

All those extras had been worth the exorbitant cost.

Out in the forest, the hum of the city and noise of cars disappeared, and at night, if you could find an open spot between the branches, the dark sky was illuminated with thousands of stars.

Cell phones didn't really work. The choices were drive about an hour onto the main road or climb the highest tree around. Even then it was iffy.

Not a place for a lady like Brandy. Perfect place for a predator looking to set a trap.

But did Brandy get it? Nope. She'd texted him numerous times over the last three days. How did he know despite the lack of signal? He went out of his way to check his phone, scraping his fingers on bark as he climbed high. Had Ulric not told her the signal was shit?

Brandy's messages started out nice. *Miss u already*. She included a few emojis, including a peach. Fucking thing made him hard.

The next few remained light and let him know what was going on.

Staying at Maeve's place for a few days. Something wrong with my water. Would love it if you swung by.

I just had the most amazing food from this little hole in the wall. Can't wait to share it with you.

Bright and peppy messages that he ignored.

The tone shifted on day three.

While some women would have gotten angry and nasty, Brandy got nicer.

I know I scare you, but here's the thing. Get over it because I am not going away.

Ignoring me won't work.

STOP IGNORING ME!!!

Don't worry, baby, I'm not giving up on you.

Surely, she jested. He'd made himself very clear. He didn't want her around. At the same time, she'd been fairly certain they were meant to be something more.

Not if he could avoid it.

On the fourth day, late afternoon, he took a moment to check in on his phone. No messages. Not even a nasty one from Brandy. Had she given up on him? Probably for the best.

His hand tightened around his phone, and it made an ominous cracking sound. He tucked it away and went to check his snares, both the ones for edible meat and the others that acted as warnings. So far none of them had been triggered. So much for drawing his enemy out into the open. He'd seen absolutely no one since his arrival. Not even a hint or a scent. The squirrels chattered all day long, and nothing startled the flocks of birds into fleeing.

With nothing to do, Billy got to reflect. Reflect on how he'd left Brandy.

What they'd done.

How he wanted to do it again.

But she probably hated him, seeing as how the cum hadn't even dried before he was gone.

I'm a dick. And that was why she'd stopped texting him.

Rather than dwell on it, he ruminated while fishing for his dinner. He'd been having great luck with the river running through his property—bought for a song, given it had no amenities and no future plans to ever get any. He was returning to his cabin with a fat walleye when he noticed the bright yellow car between the trees. He slowed his step and approached the cabin cautiously. It seemed unlikely his enemy would simply drive up to his place.

Perhaps someone who'd gotten lost?

He neared the rental vehicle with the distinct logo emblazoned on the license plate holder with a cautious step, keeping an eye and ear out. When Brandy appeared from around the side of the cabin, clutching wildflowers, his jaw dropped.

"Brandy? What the fuck are you doing here?"

"Looking for you, obviously. I've been waiting forever for you to show up. Good thing your cabin was unlocked."

"Why the fuck did you come looking for me?" He couldn't quell his language or shock.

"Did anyone ever tell you ghosting a woman after

you've had sex is the height of rudeness, Billy Gruff? You're lucky I know you enjoyed it and are just being a dumbass, or I might have been offended."

He blinked as he tried to digest her words. "I told you we couldn't see each other anymore."

"As if I don't get a say." She sniffed.

"You shouldn't be here."

"Are you going to be like Ulric and say I have no place in the woods? Because I'll have you know I love nature," she exclaimed, swinging her arms wide. Only to scream and wave them wildly. "Wasp! Wasp! Kill it!"

"I think you already did with that shriek." He winced, and she pursed her lips.

"Thanks for your help. Now that you're done being adorably sarcastic, why not grab some bags from the trunk?"

"Oh no I'm not because you're not staying."

"Don't be silly. Yes, I am. You and I have unfinished business."

"No, we don't."

"The bite mark on my boob says otherwise."

"An accident. It means nothing."

"Yeah, I can tell. It meant so little you ran away and told your friends not to tattle."

"Obviously someone did, or you wouldn't be here. They'll be hearing about it when I get back," was his dark reply.

"Don't start with your macho crap. It was Ulric, and he didn't have a choice when your plan failed."

"Wait, what? Did something happen? Are you okay?" He scanned her for injury.

"I'm fine, but it was close. Some guy with an electric saw came after me. As well as some bats."

"Can you repeat that more slowly?"

"So last night a bunch of bats—"

He interrupted. "Bats as in baseball?"

"No, the flying kind. Bat-bats." She flapped her hands. "Anyhow, they slammed into the windows of Griffin and Maeve's apartment. A couple are gonna need replacing. Swear they wanted to kill me, but a good thing they tried because it sent me down to the main floor, which is how I saw the guy trying to get in through the window."

"Even if he broke it, the windows are barred."

"Yeah, well, apparently, this saws-it-all thing isn't just noisy. It cuts through metal."

"Wait, he came with a Sawzall?"

"Yup. And he's like slicing at the bars, and I was all 'Holy shit, what am I going to do?'"

"Where was Ulric and the others?" he growled as he began to grasp the depth of the danger she'd been in.

"Ulric left to drive his aunt to some card shark party and Quinn got stuck on the 417—"

"You were alone!" He roared so loud birds in the nearby trees suddenly took flight.

Brandy didn't appear as impressed. "Yes, I was alone. Like I usually am when not at work and not the important part of the story."

"They were supposed to watch over you until I handled the threat."

"In case you missed it, misogyny is very last century, and I am just as capable as a man of taking care of myself."

"You handled a guy breaking in with a Sawzall?"

"I did."

"How? Did Ulric load you up with a gun?" Surprising, given most of his pack considered weapons to be cheating in a fight.

"Who needs a gun when you have a whacking chair?" She demonstrated by pretending to swing an invisible chair back and forth. "I took him out as he was climbing through the hole he made."

"You confronted him instead of running away?" he bellowed.

"Not sure where you think I should have gone." She sniffed in obvious annoyance.

"How about anywhere you don't need to concuss a power-tool-wielding maniac?"

"Bah. You worry too much. I told you, I handled it. A little too well. Ulric had to get rid of the body." Her lips turned down.

Immediately, contrition hit him. "Oh, baby, I'm sorry that happened to you. That must have been traumatic." Almost as traumatic as the "baby" that slipped from his mouth.

"You know, Ulric said the same thing, but honestly, I'm good. I worked in the ER for years. Dead bodies don't bother me anymore. I don't have any sympathy for a jerk who thinks it's okay to come after a defenseless woman."

"Hardly defenseless by the sound of it."

She grinned ear to ear, so pleased with herself. "Right? Only Ulric didn't see it that way. He gave me shit. Told me I should have locked myself in the upstairs bathroom until he arrived." She rolled her eyes.

"It would have been safer."

"Again, the misogyny is a little annoying. Can't anyone say, 'Good job, Brandy, you took out the bad guy'?"

"Good job, Brandy. Still not sure why you're here."

"Isn't it obvious from my story? Your not-so-brilliant plan backfired. The bad guy didn't follow you. He came after me. Which apparently was a really bad idea for him. But in good news, the coast is clear. You can come home."

"We don't know that for sure. Could be the fellow you chaired was robbing the pot shop and not related to my troubles at all," Billy argued.

"Brap." She made a noise. "Wrong. Not only did he mention looking for me, he was also an ex-convict put in jail by the one and only Detective Gruff." She gave a cheer as if there were a crowd.

"Fuck me." Billy rubbed his face.

"That is my sincere hope, Billy Gruff. Especially since I purposely left my pajamas at home."

13

After that bombshell of a statement, Brandy sauntered in the direction of his cabin while he picked up his jaw off the ground.

"Where are you going? You can't stay." Not now that she'd put the idea of the two of them fucking in his head.

She paused at the entrance to his cabin. "I'm here. Deal with it." She walked in like she owned the place and left the door open, assuming he'd follow.

He should go back into the woods. Instead, he joined her inside and was hit by something aromatic.

"What's that I'm smelling?" he asked, his tastebuds drooling.

She pointed to his oven. "Dinner."

"You cook?"

"Only when inspired." She cast him a grin over her shoulder as she placed flowers in a glass on the table.

"You shouldn't have." It wasn't the only thing she'd done while he was in the woods. He saw her bag just inside the bedroom door, her jacket hung on a hook.

"Would it kill you to say thank you and try to admit you're happy to see me?"

He was happy to see her. And it killed him. "You're leaving first thing in the morning." While he wanted her gone, it was already late. The roads were tricky at night, and, well, she had gone through the trouble of cooking and he wasn't one to waste food.

He washed up while she puttered, looking adorable in her knit sweater that hugged her hips encased in snug jeans. She'd kept her short boots on, a good idea given the damp and chilly floor. The boards could get chilly, given the cramped crawlspace didn't have any insulation.

It stunned him to realize she'd driven hours just to confront him but not in anger. That was the most baffling part. She appeared determined to ignore his rejection. On the contrary, she'd alluded to them having sex again.

It would be a mistake. He'd lost control once already. And while he didn't believe in any mystical crap about mating bites, that had never happened before.

As she set the table, she pointed to a bottle on the counter. "I completely forgot to uncork the wine. Would you?"

He eyed the wine. Red. A vintage he didn't know,

mostly because he stuck to beer. "Um, I don't have a wine opener," he admitted.

She glanced at him over her shoulder. "I knew Ulric said the place was rustic, but surely you have something we can use to uncork it?"

He shrugged.

She sighed. "It's a good thing I'm a woman of many talents. I'll need a screwdriver and a hammer."

"You're kidding, right?"

She grabbed the bottle, and a corner of her mouth lifted. "Do you really think this is the first time I've had to improvise?

He did have the tools needed ,and in short order, she'd poured them mugs of wine since his fancy glass was being used by the flower.

"You could use a few things to make the place a little homier," she remarked as she took a sip.

Billy didn't touch his. The last time they drank wine, they'd slept together. "It's not meant to be homey." He sometimes didn't even stay inside when he visited, drawn by the lure of sleeping outside with just a sleeping bag to keep him warm.

"It could be such a love nest. Add a few fat pillows on the floor. Hang a few lights that aren't trying to kill bugs at the same time."

"Sounds more like a chalet," he grumbled.

"Exactly." She beamed.

Ding.

She clapped her hands. "Have a seat and prepare to be wowed. Dinner's ready!" she sang.

Billy sat down and inhaled the fragrant scent of cooked meat with spices. He couldn't wait to dig in. Brandy pulled a platter from his propane oven and placed it on the table.

He recoiled. "Is that meatloaf?" His stomach clenched as his childhood rose up to tighten his throat.

"My specialty." She beamed, but it faded as she noticed his face. "What's wrong? You're not allergic to gluten, are you? Because I used breadcrumbs in the meat. Also onions, spices, and bacon."

All of which sounded delicious, only he shook his head. "Not allergic, I just don't eat meatloaf."

"Why not?"

"Because I don't like it."

Her nose wrinkled. "But you haven't even tried it. I swear, it's good." She put a hand on her heart even as her lips turned down.

He'd disappointed her, and it bothered him. "My mom used to make it." He could have slapped a hand over his mouth as he revealed a tiny bit of himself.

"And seeing it makes you miss her."

"Not exactly."

"You don't eat meatloaf because hers was so damned good that no one else's can compare." She tried another theory.

Another wrong one so he clarified. "My mom

couldn't cook worth shit, and her meatloaf was especially nasty."

She pursed her lips. "So you're refusing to eat my meatloaf because you were traumatized by bad food as a child?"

"Yes." Because he wasn't about to admit that it reminded him of a time he wanted to forget.

"Suck it up, buttercup. You're having a piece of mine."

"But I—"

"Don't have a choice. Stop being a baby and get ready to have your tastebuds dance."

She lopped off a hunk and drizzled some kind of gravy over it. She added mashed potatoes too.

It actually didn't hurt him to admit, "That looks delicious. It's been ages since I had a home-cooked meal."

"Mostly home cooked. The mash is from a box where you just add milk and water. It's easier, and honestly, I like them better. I hate lumpy potatoes."

"So do I."

She'd even made green beans in some kind of brown sugar mix that gave it a slight crunch. The bread was bakery fresh that day.

As for the meatloaf... "This is fucking good." It didn't stick in his throat. It went down piece after delicious piece. He even had seconds and couldn't wait to slap some on the leftover bread for lunch tomorrow.

They'd not spoken much while they shoveled food

and drank wine—because, yes, he joined her. The red went well with the meal.

He cleared the plates and ran hot water to soak them. As she washed, and he dried— mostly since he knew where shit went—they spoke.

"Who was the guy who attacked the shop?" he asked.

"Ulric didn't say, just confirmed the connection to the other convicts that attacked me."

"I can't believe he didn't tell me." His lips turned down.

"How do you know he didn't? It's not like you've been getting your messages, or you would have surely replied. Right?" That pointed glare ensured he'd take that secret to the grave.

Dishes done, they sat adjacent to each other in the worn, plaid-covered chairs. Brandy handed him a fresh mug of wine and cheered him with hers. They'd not yet finished the first bottle.

Maybe he'd be able to stick to his determination this time. Just keep things casual.

He managed an awkward, "How you been?"

She arched a brow. "Well, I was displaced from my home and separated from my cat, seeing as how someone forced me to relocate while he ran away to his fort in the woods."

"I did that to draw danger away from you."

"Which failed and has been handled. So what's the new plan now that I've saved you from the bad guy?"

"We don't know if that was the last one."

"You going to live like a doomer the rest of your life?"

"No, but there's no harm in being cautious a while longer. I'll figure something out once I get you somewhere safe."

She snorted. "Good luck with that. I did not drive hours in a rental for you to dump me on someone else."

"You can't stay here with me."

"Why not?"

He waved his hand. "As you can see, the place isn't big and lacks creature comforts."

"Don't need much. Besides the most important thing is already here."

"What?"

"You."

The surprising admission took him a moment to reply to. "I am sorry, Brandy, but as I keep telling you, we can't be a couple."

"Why not?"

"Because."

"Because is not an answer. You're afraid. Your past has made you relationship shy. Good thing for you I'm not afraid of my feelings or a challenge."

"I'm not the right guy for you."

"Pretty sure that's for me to decide."

"Don't I get a say?"

She curved her lips as she replied, "No."

"Anyone ever tell you that you're bossy?"

"Yes. And you're ornery."

"I wouldn't be ornery if you listened to what I was saying."

"Your mouth spouts one thing, but your eyes, your body..." She eyed him. "Those say something else entirely."

"Oh?"

"You want me, Billy Gruff. And it scares you."

To deny either would be a lie, so instead, he changed the subject. "Since you're staying the night, you can have the bed." He offered despite knowing the couch wouldn't fit his frame.

Laughter bubbled from her lips. "You're so adorable when you're being chivalrous. But let's get one thing clear so we can avoid any nonsense. You're sleeping with me."

"No, I'm not."

"You're right, you're not, because we'll be awake having epic sex."

"Uh." His brilliant reply.

"Thank you for not denying it. I know I'm not your dream girl—"

"Shut up. You know you're hot."

"If I were so hot, you wouldn't have ghosted me."

He tried to explain. "It's not you. It's me. And before you argue, it's not me being grumpy. I honestly don't want a relationship."

She rolled her eyes. "Then let's not have one."

"Says the woman who claims we're going to have sex."

"We can have sex and not be a couple you know. People do that all the time. It's called friends with benefits. We keep our own places. Bang when we're horny. Act as the plus-one when occasions call for it. Plus, in your case, you get to see your Pack without having to explain to your cop boss why you're hanging with drug dealers. Which by the way, is now a legal occupation and this kind of discrimination shouldn't be tolerated."

"You make it sound simple."

"It is, so take off your pants."

The pants remained on as he dumbly argued. "What if you get emotionally involved?"

"What if you do?" she countered.

"I've got baggage," he admitted.

"Don't we all?" she queried. "While I'd like to claim I have a perfect track record, obviously I don't, or we wouldn't even be having this conversation. For the sake of honesty, I will admit I've had my heart broken before. Guess what. I survived."

"I don't want to hurt you."

"You don't want to hurt me?" She giggled. "You know that's pretty sexist that you're assuming I'm the one who's going to fall in love. Maybe you should be worried instead about you."

"I'll never succumb." A dumb declaration that he

already knew was false. From the moment he'd met Brandy he'd been intrigued. In lust.

"Wow, it's like you want to tempt Cupid," she drawled.

"There is no love cherub."

"You don't believe in Cupid?" Brandy ogled. "Dude, it's like you want to be shot in both ass cheeks with the arrow of love."

"Never happen."

"Why? Why do you hate love?"

"It's more like I don't believe in it." When she kept staring, he sighed. "My parents were supposed to be in love. But it was toxic. Constant fighting. Cursing. Violence. Every day."

"That must have been hard," she said softly. "But what they had wasn't love. In my world, love was my grandparents at their fiftieth anniversary, dancing cheek to cheek. My dad bringing my mom flowers randomly just because he wanted to. My mom putting notes in the lunches she made him every day."

"Sounds like you were lucky."

"What makes you think you couldn't have the same thing?"

"For one, I'm not a regular man."

"I'm aware. What of it? I happen to like dogs. Even overgrown ones that howl at the moon."

"I'm fixed."

"I thought we already discussed the fact I'm not really into kids. I'll stick to fur babies."

"Speaking of pets, what about your kitten?"

"Ulric is babysitting Froufrou." She grinned as she added, "You should see the picture he sent of her napping under his beard."

It shouldn't have made him jealous. Blame the fact he'd gotten used to the kitten using him as her pillow.

"Why me?" was his last argument.

She stepped closer and grabbed his shirt to drag him to her. "Because you're the one who makes my panties wet. Now, are you going to toss me on that bed, or are we doing it here in your kitchen?"

"Brandy—"

She silenced him with a kiss.

He didn't have the strength to push her away. He'd argued, even as he wanted what she offered. He tried to do right by her, but in the end, he was weak. Weak for her.

He stripped her where she stood and carried her to the bed, high enough he could stand and, with her ass perched on the edge, slide into her and fuck her. Fucked her hard and fast, which might have been embarrassing if she'd not come screaming first. A good thing since he quickly followed.

They washed then got dirty again. Blame her. She existed.

Once more, he sank into her while lip locked, this time setting a slower pace that had her grunting and panting as her orgasm came in a slow but intense roll that squeezed him dry.

After that, they snuggled in front of his woodstove with its crackling fire, lying atop a bear rug that came with the place when he bought it. She read a novel with bright colors she'd brought, which she called a romantic comedy. He read a recent spy thriller.

A peaceful evening such as he'd never imagined. Never craved until he experienced it for himself.

They went to bed together and slept intertwined. Not a couple, just two people enjoying each other.

What did it say that he, the man who said no to relationships, wanted it to last forever?

14

Brandy woke snuggled against a hunk of man.

Stubborn.

Overprotective.

Gentle.

Loving.

And always horny.

She reached down to grab him, and he chuckled. "While I appreciate the thought, that isn't the kind of wood you're looking for."

"Way to ruin my fantasy of being super desirable even with bed head."

He nuzzled her hair and murmured, "You're too desirable all the time. That's the problem."

He rolled out of the bed and rather than hit the small bathroom, which he said was on a septic, chose to pee outside.

She used the toilet. Brushed her teeth while she

was in there. She emerged wearing just his shirt, which hit her mid-thigh. He stood at the stove heating up a skillet. He cast her a glance over a broad shoulder. "Eggs and bacon sound good?"

"I'd prefer sausage." And, yes, she let her gaze dip.

"I've already started cooking." He sounded so sad.

She laughed. "Maybe I'll have that sausage for dessert then."

He grinned, looking more relaxed than she recalled. So much for his claim he didn't want a relationship.

"What's on the agenda after breakfast? Maybe something to work off the calories?" She knew what kind of exercise she'd like.

However, Billy, on a quest to scare her off, didn't give her pulse-pounding sex; he got her doing chores. After they cleaned up their breakfast, they headed outside to a beautiful sunny day.

She breathed deep. Sneezed. Then chuckled. "I think I'm allergic to fresh air."

"You don't have to stay," he suggested.

She blew him a raspberry. "Nice try. What's first on the list?" She'd show him!

"I was going to chop some wood."

"Ooh, hitting things with an axe. Sounds like fun." Despite his skeptical expression, she grabbed hold of the axe and began swinging at the chunks of wood. It was harder than it looked. The tool was heavy and had a tendency to get stuck or sometimes bounce.

She lasted only a few swings before he took the axe from her. "I'll split. You stack. Last thing we need is for you to cut off a limb."

After they replenished the wood pile, he took her fishing. The worm part was gross, and she insisted he put it on the hook, but she quite enjoyed the exhilaration of her first catch.

It reeled from the water, a squirming little fishy. "I did it!" she crowed.

"Good job. It will make a decent lunch."

"Excuse me?" Shocked, she grabbed it from his hands and tossed it back in the lake.

"Why'd you do that?"

"You can't eat Herman."

"You named the fish?"

"Seemed only right given he was my first." She winked.

He grumbled, so she kissed him. Pressed her mouth to his, and while he might protest, he didn't push her away. On the contrary, he took her on the thick grass by the lakeshore. Then again on their walk back to the cabin, her back against a tree.

By dinner time, he'd abandoned all talk of her leaving. They also avoided speaking of the future. Eventually, they'd have to define what was unfolding between them, but not yet. Not until she showed him what a life together could be like. Billy's stubborn nature ensured she had her work cut out for her. But do it she would, if only to prove to Billy Gruff that he could be happy.

With her.

Despite what she'd claimed, she wanted more than just some casual hookups. Something about Billy screamed "just right," and she wasn't the type to give up easily.

After a dinner of steaks with baked potatoes—which he cooked on his barbecue—she stood and said, "That was delicious. But I'm still hungry." She crooked a finger.

"I really should be doing my rounds and checking the traps."

"Can't it wait a few minutes?" she asked as she removed the shirt she wore and dropped it to the floor. She cast him a sloe-eyed look over her shoulder as she swished her hips on the way to his bed.

Before she even reached it, he came up behind her and cupped her breasts. His hot breathed fanned against her neck and earlobe as he growled, "Why must you drive me so crazy?"

"Because it's what I do best."

He pushed her over, propping her ass so that he could slide into her. The angle wasn't the best for her, and he knew it. He tugged her over to his chair, sitting down first then dragging her into his lap.

His fingers found her clit as he thrust into her, grinding and pulling her hard onto his lap as she rocked. She dug her fingers into his shoulders as she took what he offered and gave back, lifting and dropping herself on him until she panted and mewled. He took over then, his strong hands on her hips dragging her back and forth, the friction on her clit nothing compared to the pressure on her sweet spot. She came. Hard.

He kissed her temple. "You gonna live, baby?"

"Barely. Maybe give me some mouth-to-mouth?"

He chuckled. "I start that, and I'll never get out of here."

He was right. They ended up staying in. The next morning, the rain also kept them inside. In bed. Naked.

It was middle of the afternoon before Billy dressed to go check his traps. She chopped up some ingredients for dinner, their supply of edibles getting low. They'd have to venture out of their nest to get some food soon, but she dreaded it, fearful they'd shatter what they'd been building the last few days.

"You coming or staying?" he asked as he tugged on his boots.

"I thought I already came," she teased. "But I'm game to go again."

"Leave me some skin on my dick, would ya?" He came close enough to lean in for a kiss. "If we're lucky, I'll bring home some meat for tomorrow's dinner."

"You could always eat me," she offered.

"Mmm. I just might. For dessert." He winked.

This playful side pleased her enormously. "These traps of yours, are they far?"

"Some are, but I was only going to check the closest."

She couldn't resist a chance to spend time with him, seeing him in his element. "Give me a second to put some clothes on."

"You're coming?" He sounded surprised. "What about the food?"

"I can finish it when I get back."

"Dress warm. It can get chilly in the woods, especially when the sun hides behind clouds."

She pulled on her jeans, a T-shirt, a sweater, then her coat, which she left open. Warm socks and her boots completed the ensemble. Billy waited for her just outside in worn jeans, a plaid lumberjacket, and a baseball cap. He also had a rifle strung over his shoulder. The other shoulder held a knapsack.

"Ready?" he asked.

She nodded. Silly her, she'd expected some idyllic meander through forest paths that led to a flower-filled clearing. The reality involved tree roots and slippery piles of fallen leaves. Holes that tried to break her ankle. Branches that attacked her hair and slapped her in the face. Billy did his best to help, catching her before she fell. Sometimes even catching the limbs looking to whip her delicate skin.

As for the flowery clearings where she'd expected them to make love? Scraggly grass and prickly weeds filled them.

Her nose wrinkled.

"What's wrong?" he asked.

"The movies really had me expecting something

different. And warmer." The damp chill kept trying to settle in her bones.

"Do you want to go back?"

He only offered because she was being a wuss. Proving Ulric's claim that she wasn't outdoorsy, but Billy was, and impressing Billy remained her top priority.

"I'm fine. Lead the way." She waved a hand, even as she wondered how much longer her poor little feet could keep going. Her boots were meant for rainy days in the city, not traipsing in the woods.

The checking of traps proved unexciting, as they were all empty, unlike the sky that filled with dark clouds.

She eyed them with trepidation. "That doesn't look good."

He grabbed her by the hand. "I know a place we can ride out the storm."

By now she'd probably go anywhere he told her unless it involved going away from him. Spending time with Billy had her only more certain than ever they were meant to be mates.

Lovers.

Partners for life.

Buddies in the woods.

Which she wasn't sold on yet.

The only thing they had going for them walked by her side.

He brought them to a cave that held the remains of a firepit, the smell of its smoke permeating the air.

"I take it you've camped here before."

He nodded. "It's a good spot in hunting season. Lots of deer in this area."

"I don't know if I could eat it."

"You eat meat already. Venison is meat."

A mindset she'd have to attempt. She'd grown up eating the basics. Venturing from her comfort zone wasn't easy.

"Are you planning to live here full time?"

"No."

A surprise reply. "Why not?"

"Because, if you hadn't noticed, it's quite remote. Even I need some kind of companionship."

"Oh." She cocked her head. "Is it hard not being part of your pack?"

"Yes. But the thing is I know the minute I choose to leave the force, there will be a place for me."

"And is there a place in your life for me?" she asked.

His mouth opened and shut before he settled on, "I thought this was just casual sex."

"Did you actually say that with a straight face?"

"You told me that was all this was."

"And you believed that?" She could see by his face he wanted it to be true. Didn't want to admit he might just be emotionally involved. So she proved it. "Maybe I should leave. After all, if you're not going to give me what I want, why waste my time? Plenty of men out there. Men who'd like a woman who can make a mean meatloaf."

"No!" He practically roared the word.

"Why not? You don't care about me," she taunted.

"Why are you doing this?" He grabbed Brandy and dragged her close.

"Because you can't keep pretending."

"Why not?" he grumbled.

"Because I deserve better."

That froze him, and for a moment, she thought she'd lost him. Instead his mouth crushed hers in a kiss that only cemented what she knew.

I love you.

Unfortunately, she said it aloud.

15

It was a wet walk back to the cabin. A quiet one, too, since Brandy dropped that bombshell.

She loves me.

It probably slipped past her lips by accident. A casual expression. She didn't actually mean it.

At the cabin, he cleared his throat. "You should get changed out of those wet things."

She paused in the doorway. "Aren't you coming in?"

"I will in a bit. I didn't check the east side, and I really should. I'll be back before dinner. Lock the door. Don't open for anyone. Use the airhorn if anyone does show up."

Warnings and protection because he couldn't stay. He unabashedly fled. Had to since he needed time to evaluate how to handle the situation. He'd never had a woman declare herself.

Never wanted it. Would have been appalled.

But...

This was Brandy. The woman who'd slipped into his life and bed and made it so he couldn't picture either without her.

And he couldn't handle it. So he fled with a feeble excuse.

The traps showed no signs of being tampered with. On the contrary, he saw no signs of any living things around. No animal tracks, no bird sounds, just the hum of bugs who weren't daunted by anything.

It could be the night silenced naturally. These woods boasted predators other than human and Lycan, bears being the most common, but even a large, aggressive buck or a moose—whose sheer size alone made them daunting—could have passed through.

He smelled nothing. His human nose wasn't exactly ideal for fine sniffing, and yet he had no idea how to change into his wolf without the moon's influence, nor did he want to. The lack of control wasn't something to be encouraged.

However, in this moment, his inability to properly smell disturbed. The world around felt unnatural without the usual smells. He crouched to the ground, his fingers skimming the damp, fallen leaves. It helped to ground him. He debated his next course of action. The various booby traps he'd set remained untriggered. Fine spider webs strung between trees. Leaves were left in a particular pattern. Not all traps caused harm.

Some were for warning. He should have been reassured that not a single one was triggered. Instead, it roused his cautious side.

What if someone hunted these woods? Someone smart enough to evade all the subtle snares. Someone possibly one step ahead of him.

Panic hit him, not for himself. He'd left Brandy alone in the cabin. The door was locked. It wouldn't stand long against someone determined, but every second counted in a fight.

I shouldn't have left her. At the same time, he knew she'd not only kick his ass for suggesting she was too fragile to stay by herself but he'd kick his own ass for not following his own rules of engagement.

Check the perimeter. Make sure it remained unbreached. There were only two ways to get into this place. One by trekking days in the wilderness, which included a mountain, a river, and marsh that even he would never attempt. Or by driving in on that one and only road. A road he could hear from at least a mile away on a still day. The wind had died completely, leaving the moisture in the air heavy, pressed down by the gray and angry clouds overhead.

I should turn around.

He should stop being so dramatic. Gone less than an hour and no sign of danger. He remained close enough to hear if she called out for him. The question being, would she? Brandy didn't mind a fight. A tough woman with a mushy heart. They were only two of the many things he loved about her.

Choke.

Gasp.

Billy wavered on his feet, suddenly dizzy.

It couldn't be love. He wasn't supposed to love.

And yet... If he tried to imagine a tomorrow without Brandy in it, it just seemed bleak and useless. She'd brought some sunshine to his life, and now that he basked in its warmth, he didn't want to lose it.

Maybe that explained the tension in him. The conviction that something was wrong in a forest that had offered no kind of threat, and yet his gut remained tight.

Fuck it. He'd been out here long enough, not to mention his whole reason for fleeing— her declaration of love—now seemed a moot point as he finally admitted to himself what he should have known all alone.

I love Brandy Herman.

He angled for the cabin, his pace rapid, his head swinging side to side, looking for any hint of movement or color in this gray-lit space.

Pit. Pat. Plop. A fat wet drop rolled from a leaf to his nose as the rain began. The patter as it hit leaves just the precursor to when it would roll and join together to form large raindrops that hit like wet bombs. Cold bombs.

Billy shivered as he passed the bole of the massive

oak that he'd nicknamed Titan. His pace slowed, and he glanced from the gnarled bark at the base with ridges to stand on then upwards to the spreading boughs. Limbs thick enough to hold a man. But if Billy climbed, and luck chose to be on his side, even on a cloudy day he might get a bar on his phone.

He'd not checked in since... When had he last loaded his messages? He'd been so distracted since her arrival. He should make sure nothing had happened.

Despite the light rain, he gripped the trunk of the tree and began to climb. Gripping the ridged exterior of the massive tree, he reached a branch, and from there he had to mostly make large steps to keep climbing as high as he dared. Only then did he stand, head and shoulders poking through wet leaves, the rivulets of water soaking him. Rain plinked across his crown and face as he poked slightly from the boughs, not fully at the top of the tree, but still higher than most of the forest.

He dug into his zippered inner pocket. It was weatherproof and also contained matches, a flint, and fifty bucks. The phone had most of its battery since he kept it fully turned off. Not only did that prevent tracking by someone clever with a satellite, it preserved the battery.

The phone powered up, and when it hit the log-in screen, he entered his passcode. No thumbprint or facial lock for him. He wanted something that required him coherent and willing. The home screen showed nothing new, given the reception icon at the top of the phone flashed as it sought a signal. When it finally steadied, he'd achieved a puny—barely a bar—3G.

He really should look into getting a dish put in. Maybe some more solid security, too, in the form of hunter cams. The kind that were hooked to cellular and ran on solar. Almost instant pictures or video.

As to why the sudden interest in upgrading? Brandy. A city girl like her might want some amenities. Internet access being one of the easier ones if he invested. It would be nice to have the ability to stream a movie on a dark and stormy night.

His phone began to ping as emails piled up in his box, as did a few text messages.

He could read those later if necessary. He had a single bar, who to call?

Before he'd even finished formulating the question in his mind he was scrolling for Ulric's number. Not only would Ulric be the best informed, Billy could also give him shit for letting Brandy travel out here by herself. That could have been so dangerous. Not only for accidents—because out here, the wildlife could get big—but because she could have been abducted along the way. Even if that guy in the city had been taken care of, that didn't mean there weren't others out to hurt Billy by any means possible.

Ring. His phone rang three, four times. The line clicked, and Billy expected to be sent to voicemail. Instead, Ulric answered.

"Detective Gruff. What a pleasant surprise."

Odd greeting. Did Ulric have someone listening in?

"Like I said at the wedding, call me Billy." He played along for the moment.

A voice blared, and Ulric grumbled, "Excuse the background noise. I'm at the grocery store."

Ah. That explained why Ulric spoke cautiously. "Sounds fun."

"More like necessity. I guess now that you're dating the boss's wife's best friend, we'll be seeing you around the shop more often."

"Yeah, they've already threatened me with couples night."

"Speaking of couples, how is Brandy? I haven't heard a peep since she left to join you. I'm going to assume she made it to the boonies."

"Brandy is good. We're having a great time. It's nice having the woods all to ourselves. The city can be so chaotic. But that's not why I'm calling. She's been worried about her damned cat but can't call since getting signal is a pain in the ass unless you're willing to drive an hour or climb a tree."

Ulric coughed. "Are you in a tree?"

"Yes."

That resulted in a well-deserved snicker. "You must really like her."

Billy blushed, by himself, up a fucking a tree. "Um,

this is just about easing her mind about the cat. How is the little bugger?"

"Her highness is doing fantastic. She's taken quite a liking to my bedroom. Especially my pillow."

"Must be fun sleeping."

"I've been trying naps on the couch at regular intervals that coincide with her feeding schedule. It's been working out well because now I remember to put food out before she wakes from her naps hangry and scratchy."

Billy offered a dry, "You do realize you outweigh the cat by over two hundred pounds."

"I do and am impressed by her highness' ability to ensure I obey her every command. It's kind of scary if I'm honest." Ulric sounded sincere, and Billy wanted to laugh, but he hadn't called for entertainment.

Knowing Ulric was in public, Billy tempered his speech. "I hear there was an attempted break-in the other night." He didn't worry about mentioning it because it was the type of thing that Brandy would have told him about, especially since it couldn't be easily hidden. Sawed-off security bars and a broken window would be noticeable even if repaired quickly.

"Yeah. We got video before he smashed the cameras. We had enough footage of the culprit for the cops to identify the guy. Franklin Gregor. An ex-con. Just got out of jail. I'm surprised you didn't hear." Ulric's voice dropped an octave as he dropped a salacious, "Apparently, he was friends with those two dudes that pulled those guns at the cop station last week."

The name only confirmed what Brandy told him. He recalled Franklin Gregor. He'd busted him with his meth lab, luckily before it went kaboom.

If ever someone deserved jail time it was Gregor. A real piece of shit, he'd been arrested too many times to easily list, starting in his teens. Attacking Brandy, working with others to do violence? Billy totally believed it; however, he doubted Gregor would be the brains running any kind of vendetta. He didn't have the personality to get even a roach to join in his cause. In prison, Gregor would have been a follower, along with the other two. Which left the question, who was their alpha?

Not just wolves had them. In the human world, there were people, mostly male, who had a way of convincing people to follow them. Just look at any dictator and their fervent soldiers or cults and the worshippers who ingested, without qualms, their new religion.

Someone charismatic could convince others to do their bidding. In this case, hurt Billy Gruff by hurting Brandy.

Who, though?

"Damn, that's some crazy shit," Billy finally replied. "At least knowing who it is will make the guy easier to catch."

"So you'd think, and yet the cops still haven't found

him." In oblique fashion, Ulric relayed that the body had been disposed of in a way that wouldn't tie back to them.

"Pity my looking into your case would be a conflict of interest."

"Bah. We don't need no special favors. Not really worried about a petty criminal. Besides, he ran off before he managed to steal anything." Ulric paused. "When are you coming back?"

"Not sure. The weather is pretty shit. I'm debating if we should stay the rest of the week or head home tomorrow."

"Stay. The weather ain't any better here." Meaning, he thought the danger remained.

"Says the man who is trying to win over the affections of a cat." Billy turned the conversation light again.

"She already loves— Argh."

The high-pitched shriek had Billy exclaiming, "Ulric?"

"I'm fine. Just a few scratches," Ulric huffed before clearing his throat and muttering, "My own fault. I left her majesty in the car too long. In my defense, the seafood counter was busy."

"You got her cat fresh fish?"

"Only the best for the princess."

Billy chuckled. "You are so pussy whipped. I should go. The rain's getting heavier, and Brandy's making something I can smell from here." A hint of fragrant deliciousness.

"Is it her chili? She makes an epic one with lots of spice."

Don't be jealous. Billy did his best to not crush his phone as he said, "She doesn't need to cook anything to make me feel spicy."

With that, he hung up. Then gaped at himself. He'd never been that...that blasé before. Ulric must be wondering what the fuck.

What the fuck, indeed. Billy wasn't just falling in love. He was there six feet deep in it.

He climbed down the tree and hit the damp ground, noticing the stillness. While amongst the boughs, he'd been concentrating more on his phone than his environment. But now, amidst the boles wreathed in a creeping mist, an unnatural silence fell, no wind or creak of foliage. More ominous? The lack of humming bugs.

The hair on his nape lifted. Despite the lack of evidence, he'd swear he wasn't alone. He took cautious steps, heading for the cabin, even as he debated moving away. Did the person—*thing*—shadowing him know she was there?

If they did, then closer to the cabin would be more useful to Brandy. He quickened his pace, half crouched, alert. His hearing sharpened. His gaze refocused. The danger to Brandy had him pulsing inside. The beast wanted to help. Rather insistently.

Just not enough to change.

The thing about being Lycan was the wolf only

had the strength to come out for the full moon. Unless a man had an alpha inside. An alpha Lycan could shift anytime, anywhere, because the wolf was stronger than the man. A strange way of putting it, given alphas were known for their leadership qualities because they displayed character and strength. But when it came to who controlled the body, in an alpha, the Lycan within could shove its way out at need.

A wolf right now might not be the best thing to protect Brandy. Unlike his brothers who eschewed guns, Billy liked to hedge his bets. The rifle over his shoulder wasn't what he unslung though. The dagger fitted his palm quite nicely. Its balance familiar. He'd been tossing blades since he was a teen and the guys living on the ranch next door showed him how.

He ran lightly, the encroaching fog swirling and making it hard to see. It felt unnatural, a strange thing to even think, given his own Lycan heritage. Yet there remained no better way of describing it. He'd never seen such a thing other than in horror movies.

He bolted hard as he remembered all the blood and screams on screen. He couldn't let anything happen to Brandy. Apparently, he should have worried more about himself.

The bats attacked as he exited the forest into the cleared area by the cottage. He never saw them coming in the fog, the heavy blanket of it muffling sound until they were almost atop him. Even then, he just heard the odd whispery paper-snap of their wings. A few at first then more and more dove from the swirling mist, a dark wave that belonged in a nightmare.

Billy lifted his arms and did his best to shove past them. The deluge of diving bats didn't diminish. The dark swarm of them surrounded him in a funnel of moving fur, fang, and wing.

"Billy!" He heard Brandy yell much too clearly. She must have stepped out of the cabin.

"Get back inside, you idiot!" Not the nicest thing to say, but what was she thinking coming out here?

He flailed at the furry, writhing swarm and clearly heard her exclaim, "Where's a flamethrower when you need one? Got any hairspray lying around?"

"No fires," he hollered. "We're surrounded by kindling."

"Do you have chili powder?" She kept yelling as he swatted and punched the bats. Dozens, perhaps hundreds, attacked. Not very well, he should add. While they batted about his head and body, they didn't actually manage to bite or do more than land a few light scratches.

Wouldn't you know Brandy joined him, swinging a boot of all things, connecting to the furry bodies with hard smacks. She made her way to him with wide eyes.

"What's going on?" she yelled, waving her boot of deadly destruction to clear the air.

"Bat attack," he muttered. An inane answer and yet none of this made sense.

"This reminds me of when they attacked Griffin's

apartment in the city." She kept swinging, dangerously close to hitting him in the face.

"Let's get inside." The tide of bats had thinned enough that he could grab her and pull in the direction of the cabin.

They ran inside, and he slammed the door, dropping a bar over it as if it would make a difference. The windows would be the issue. He went to the biggest one, the curtains wide open. The fog outside made visibility poor, but even as he watched, it thinned just in time to see the much-diminished tide fly off over the forest. "They're gone."

"Not all of them." Brandy hugged herself as she glanced at the bodies piled on the ground.

A proper woodsman would call the government agency in charge of weird wildlife shit and have them come take samples. But that would involve lots of questions and sticking around when all he wanted to do was leave. Unnatural fog and bat attack? He wasn't about to be the dumbass in the movie who stuck around claiming everything was fine. Even as he worried about the danger if they left.

But back home, he could count on his brothers.

With a grim expression, he growled, "Pack your things. We're heading back to the city."

16

Billy had told her to pack her things, and Brandy took a moment to gape before sputtering, "Excuse me?"

"We're leaving."

"Now?"

"Yes." He walked to the dresser and opened the drawers, pulling out his things and stuffing them into the bag he yanked from under the bed.

"Because of the bats?" Which admittedly freaked her out, but at the same time, they'd not been harmed.

"Among other things. I don't like that we don't have any access to the outside world, and add in the fact that we've seen no sign of being stalked, it leads me to believe we're wasting our time."

"Well excuse me. I didn't realize the time we'd spent together was so boring."

He shot her a dark look. "You know that's not what

I meant. My number one concern is keeping you safe, and I don't think I can do that here."

"Why can't we leave in the morning? Supper's almost ready." Not that she had much appetite. She'd just played whack-a-bat, and all she won was a sour taste in her mouth and a lawn covered in rats with wings.

"How long until we can eat? I'd like to get on the road soon."

"That's a long drive to be doing at night. I don't do so good with oncoming traffic in the dark." Her nose wrinkled.

"We can stop at a motel if you want. I just want to get us away from here."

"Ooh, dirty motel sex. Now you're talking." She turned to the oven and flipped it off. She pulled out the casserole and left it to cool on the table while she packed. When she offered him some food, he took a portion and literally wolfed it down. She ate a smaller amount. Blame him for being contagious. She now found herself just as anxious to leave.

After a quick wash of the dishes, she loaded her bag in her car while glancing all around as if expecting another bat attack. Silly really. It was probably the fog or something that had them acting odd.

As she slammed the trunk shut, Billy emerged from the cabin with a cooler. "What are you doing?" he asked.

"Packing to go as ordered."

"Wrong vehicle. We're taking mine." He stowed the cooler, along with the bags he'd already brought out, in his large SUV.

She snorted. "No I'm not. You do realize this is a rental. If I don't return it, it will cost me a fortune."

"I don't want you alone."

"Then you can ride with me."

"But I need my wheels."

"And I need mine. So guess you'll be admiring my taillights."

"I don't like it," he said with a grimace.

"You don't like a lot of things," she pointed out.

His scowl went well with his short, "Fine."

In the end, he had no choice. They each got into their vehicles, and she led the way, gripping the steering wheel tight as they weaved the narrow two-lane road through a forest that appeared much more ominous at night.

At every bend in the road, she expected to see some obstacle. Tree. Animal. Body. Monster… Blame the horror movies that suddenly chose that moment to haunt her.

Given her fear of hitting a moose—which never boded well for the car—she drove the speed limit. The lonely drive made her wish she'd fought harder for him to ride with her. It was a good hour before her phone started pinging as it received messages. She'd not hooked it to the rental car, which meant she couldn't see if any were important, and stopping on the side of the road in the dark with the woods pressing in on all sides didn't seem like the smartest idea either.

But having a signal meant she could make a call. "Okay, Hal, call the Viking." She'd renamed her phone after the supercomputer in *Space Odyssey* and as for who she called…

Ulric didn't answer. His voicemail beeped, and she left a basic message. "On our way home. Stopping soon for the night. Hope Froufrou is treating you okay."

Last she'd seen her kitten, Froufrou had the blond giant wrapped around her teeny, tiny paw.

She was about to call Billy, just for a connection to another human, when he flashed his high beams from behind. She slowed as he passed her. For a second, she thought he meant to set a faster pace, but he pulled into a seedy motel, the kind where only the T remained lit and the building was just one long rectangle. She would have thought it derelict if not for the faint light coming through the blinds at the last window next to a door marked in reflective tape spelling Office.

Billy pulled in front, and she parked beside him.

"Did you make a reservation?" she asked as she got out and stretched.

"No, but given the vacant parking lot, I don't think we'll have a problem."

"Norman Bates' motel never seemed busy either because he kept killing the patrons," she muttered, hugging her body as the chill of night swept through her.

"Some of the boys have stayed here before. The owner is harmless. Shall we?" He reached for her hand, but she noticed the other one remained down by his side, his lumberjacket open and loose. She knew he wore a gun holstered by his armpit. It reassured.

A bell dinged as they entered the office. The stench of cigarettes permeated, as did the canned laugh track of a television playing somewhere.

Before Billy could slap the bell on the counter, a gangly woman emerged from a swinging door, eyes wide, dark hair pulled back in a braid.

"Evening."

"Hi." Billy flashed her a high-wattage smile. "We need a room."

The woman didn't return the smile as she flipped open a book. "Pair of doubles or a king?"

"King please."

"Cash or credit?"

"Credit."

The woman whipped out her phone and squished a portable card reader at the top, ready before Billy had even pulled out his card.

The moment the rip-off of seventy-nine dollars plus tax was subtracted, the clerk handed them a key with a number three dangling from it.

They left the office, and as he guided her toward the room, Brandy said, "Shouldn't we move the cars?"

"Nope because that would be advertising what room we're in."

"It's gonna pretty damned obvious no matter what. Or are we supposed to sit in the dark?"

He sighed. "Okay, so maybe I'm being overcautious. I'm still kind of wigged out by those bats. In all my years of going to the cabin, that's never happened."

"And it turned out to be a nothing burger. Look at us. Not a single bite. Guess I'll have to wait a while longer before I turn into a vampire."

He snorted. "Ain't no vampires in these parts."

"Wait, are you saying they do exist?"

"Maybe." He offered her a wink as he put the key in the door.

As she followed him in, she couldn't help but say, "What else is real? Mermaids? Chupacabras? Unicorns?"

"I'd say at one point all the creatures of legend existed but humanity drove them to extinction."

"Werewolves aren't extinct," she pointed out.

"Werewolves, unlike most other creatures, can hide in plain sight."

She eyed their room, a true relic from the past, replete with shag carpet that never died, just wore out in spots. Its surface was matted enough that all manner of treasure could be hidden. The bed held a thick and coarse comforter of a pattern that hurt the eyes. The blocky dark furniture had light scratches over most of its surface. The television might very well kill someone if it fell on them.

"I feel like I've stepped back in time," she muttered as stuck her head in the bathroom to admire the mustard-yellow tile offset by the pale-green toilet.

"Vintage, baby," he replied from the door. "Hungry?"

"A little bit, but I didn't see any restaurants nearby." Nor any ice cream. She would have liked to eat away her sorrow at how quickly he'd had them leave their cozy cabin in the woods. She already missed its big, comfy bed and the man she'd been getting to know. Would the lover—whose body she knew intimately—turn back into Grumpy Detective Gruff?

"I could bring the cooler in for us to scrounge."

"I doubt there's much in there we'd want to eat, given we don't have a microwave to cook."

"I'm going to take a peek around and see if I can't wrangle some food and drink."

"If that peek results in wine, I wouldn't complain."

"Is that a hint to bring a bottle from your trunk?"

She grinned. "I tossed in your screwdriver and hammer just in case."

He shook his head. "Incorrigible."

"More like ready for any occasion."

He left and returned with a bottle and the tools. He even uncorked it and poured it into a paper cup.

"Ah, nothing like roughing it," she teased, lifting it to her lips.

"I should have brought the chips from the cabin and really made it special," he added with a quirk of his lips.

"Pity there's no vending machine." Her lips turned down.

"We might not be out of luck. According to the map on my phone, there's a gas station just up the road that probably has snacks. Put your shoes back on and we'll go raid it."

"Screw that. I am sitting right here and enjoying this fine vintage." She lifted her glass in salute as she plopped into the vinyl-covered chair by the window.

"I don't like the idea of leaving you alone." He appeared torn as he glanced outside then back in at her.

"There's no one here," she remarked. "I'll be fine. It's not like you'll be gone long."

Her logic won. He drew the drapes over the window. Checked the bathroom as well before leaning down to kiss her and whisper, "Don't leave the room and lock the door when I leave."

"Don't take too long. This wine is making me hungry."

He chuckled. "You are just like your cat. Ulric said her highness—her new title by the way—has not been missing any of her meals."

"When did you talk to Ulric?"

"Just before the bats pulled that spooky shit with us."

"It must have been a signal thing. You know they fly using sonar."

"Doesn't explain the fog."

"You know what does? Google. Ask it and you will find out more than you ever wanted to know about the mist. Just don't look at anything Stephen King wrote about it."

He grimaced. "I know I sound crazy."

She nipped his chin. "More like you got a case of the heebie-jeebies. Fear not, baby, I'll protect you."

"How? I didn't bring my boots or a frying pan for you to use."

She grinned. "Don't you worry. I'll find something good for whacking."

"I'm sure you will," he teased.

He left, and Brandy scrolled through her messages that had piled up over the past few days. Maeve had sent vacation pics, looking so happy and utterly in love. Ulric had also sent his fair share of Froufrou, bringing a smile to her lips. A single unidentified call hadn't left a voicemail but had texted a single word: *Soon.*

It sent a chill, as it reminded her of the messages at the office. Delete and block. Probably a wrong number. Or was this related to what had been happening? Shit. She should tell Billy about it. Soon as he got back.

She sent off a few replies and pics of her own. Her phone might not have any signal at the cabin, but she'd taken plenty of pictures. Billy chopping wood. Billy peeling off his shirt. Billy in the woods, looking every inch the predator. Billy with a smoldering expression and melting every single part of her.

Bored and hungry, she flipped to her stomach on the bed, not interested in social media. Instead, she browsed the pictures she'd taken of her time with Billy. The cabin. Him in bed under the covers. Him cooking. They made her smile. The ones in the woods were in rougher shape, as the ambient light and general environment conspired to make some blurry.

A green blob that might have been a leaf?

Delete.

Billy holding back a branch for her?

Keep.

The next would have been a delete, given more than half of it consisted of a tree trunk only, but her attention snagged on a face farther away, peeking out from behind another wide bole, their features caught in sharp relief.

Not a face she knew. But more worrisome, it meant they'd been watched. It could be innocuous—a hiker or a hunter—and yet, it chilled her to know they'd not been alone. Oh god, had that person watched them when they had their trysts in the woods?

Billy hadn't returned yet, so she attached image to a text saying, *You were right. Someone was in the woods.* Before she could hit Send, her phone died.

She stared at it. "Are you kidding me?" It had been at twenty-one percent. "Argh." Stupid battery. She rolled from the bed and went looking for a cord. None in her purse. Her suitcase held only clothes. Dammit. She must have forgotten it in the car.

The keys jangled as she snared them from the dresser. She paused by the door. Billy told her to stay inside. At the same time, Billy would be back any minute and there was no one else here. She put her hand on the knob and recalled how they'd thought themselves alone at his cabin too.

She was being paranoid. Could be simply someone out on a nature walk or camping in the woods. It wasn't as if Billy had his property fenced in.

The car was right there. Like literally within sight of the door. Plenty of time to see someone coming.

She opened the door and stuck her head out. Only her car was parked outside. Billy must have driven to the gas station. She wedged the door to keep it open. It took her seconds to reach the car. She clicked the fob to her rental and opened the driver side door. The cord wasn't plugged into the dash. She leaned in and checked the console before glancing in the passenger foot well.

"There you are," she muttered, leaning farther to reach it. Her fingers grasped it just as she heard the crunch of gravel.

She whipped out of the car so fast she whacked her head. Blinking back tears was what saved her as headlights blinded. A vehicle rolled past slowly, and in the aftermath of the glare, she couldn't see the driver. She slammed her door shut and noticed the car stopped at the far end of the lot, leaving her with a dilemma. If she went to her room, they'd see which one. Instead, she entered the office, the jangling bell reassuring.

The television still played in the background, but the woman from before didn't come out to check. Brandy peeked through the window to see the vehicle had exited the parking lot on the far side and returned to the road.

She exhaled a sigh of relief. False panic. Then again, it had been odd. Why drive through the parking lot? Perhaps they thought the motel was closed?

Or they saw her from the road, ass up in the air, searching for a cord and thought she might be easy pickings. Whatever the case, she remained safe, and Billy would be back any second. He'd be pissed if he returned while she was wandering around.

Exiting the motel office, she bolted for her room. The door was still propped open with the metal clip she'd stuck in the crack so it wouldn't lock on her. She slammed the door shut and leaned against it.

Safe.

Then again, had she even been in any danger? She never used to be this nervous. Perhaps the recent attacks had rattled her more than she realized. Brandy always did pride herself on being capable and not easily scared. That was before she'd been choked, drugged, and abducted as well as targeted by weird-acting bats and a Sawzall-wielding maniac. She'd earned her rapidly beating pulse and clammy skin.

She eyed the bathroom. A shower would be nice, and Billy would enjoy coming in to find her slippery and wet.

She kicked off her shoes and padded into the bathroom. The shower curtain, a dark burgundy, was pulled across the tub. For a second, she hesitated, only to yank it in one fierce move.

Nothing in the green tub but rust spots.

"You're being a ninny," she chided herself.

She started the water and had her hands on the hem on her shirt when she heard something. A scratching at the door and a click of turning tumblers had her whirling, heart racing. Someone unlocked the door.

Billy was back.

She practically flew across the room to yank on the handle, eager to feel his arms around her.

Only to stare dumbly and mumble, "You're not Billy."

By the time that fact registered, she was already unconscious.

17

THE GAS STATION wasn't far from the motel, a half-mile, easily walked. Billy drove, mostly to ensure at least one of their vehicles had a full tank. Prudent in case they had to leave quickly.

Did he think they were in danger? He couldn't tell. The intuitive detective found himself muddled, mostly because his concern over Brandy overshadowed all rationale. There'd been nothing in the woods that he'd found. No signs of anyone or anything passing through. He'd fled because of oddly behaving bats and a gut feeling. A gut twisted in knots because he'd still not addressed the whole love thing with Brandy.

He pulled into the gas station and began filling his car. While it slowly chugged, he pulled out his phone and dictated a quick search. *Bat swarm*. Mostly references to movies and books. He pursed his lips. *Bats acting weird*. Also a useless search. *Bat radar malfunc-*

tioning. That got some interesting hits. He skimmed an article about something called echolocation jamming. It was when an animal had its sonar interfered with. It led to them being disoriented and acting out of sorts. Just like those bats.

Brandy was right. He'd let his fear send them fleeing into the night. How emasculating. At the same time, he needed to back to the city before his leave of absence became more permanent.

His car took an unseemly amount of gas, which then led to sticker shock at the price. Stupid carbon tax. It had made a dent in his wallet since it came in effect. Despite the hike, he had no plans on changing his driving habits or vehicle. They'd pry his gas-guzzling SUV out of his dead, decidedly poorer, hands.

His phone pinged. His screen showed a text from Ulric. *Call me. I know you've got signal. Line is being secured.*

Serious shit, meaning he couldn't delay but he also couldn't dally paying for the gas or the clerk would call it in. Billy chose to not prepay at the pump because he'd intended to go inside and stock up on snack foods and drink. He'd do that quickly and then call Ulric.

As Billy headed inside, his phone rang. A glance showed an impatient Ulric.

He answered as he entered the chip isle. "Hey, what's up?"

"Good thing you ignored me and got out of Dodge. Shit's happened since we last talked."

"I would hardly call that a conversation."

"Not my fault you called at a bad time."

"What happened?"

"First, I am going to assume Brandy is with you."

"More or less. She's waiting for me in the motel room." Hopefully wearing very few clothes. "I was just getting us some snacks up the road."

"Oh fuck. You need to get back to her."

He put back the bag of chips he'd just grabbed. His gut tightened. "What's going on?"

"Remember how those dudes causing trouble were all recently released from prison?"

"Yeah."

"Turns out there's been an incident at said prison. The news only picked up on it about an hour ago."

"I take it some of them escaped?"

"Yes. They don't know for sure yet how many or who. They're still sorting through the bodies."

Bodies as in plural. "Hold on, you saying some convicts murdered their way out?"

"This was more than people killing to escape. It was staff and inmates alike. Torn apart as if attacked by an animal. The blood licked clean."

At the shocking news, Billy weaved his way through the aisles to the cash register. He just wanted to pay and leave. Running in a panic would only lead to unwanted attention.

"Give me a second," he murmured to Ulric.

The young fellow behind the counter remained fixated on his phone.

Billy cleared his throat. "I need to pay for the gas."

"Yup." The guy punched something on his register. Billy pulled out his wallet.

The door behind him opened. Not unusual—it was a gas station after all—but the clerk's wide eyes as he backed away.

Oh shit. Billy whirled and had only a millisecond to react, as the person who'd just walked in raised a shotgun. Billy ducked as it blasted then lunged, tackling the shooter around the legs.

To his surprise the guy behind the counter not only yanked the shotgun out of the shooter's grip but he pressed it against the man's forehead and spat, "You dumb fuck. What did I tell you would happen if you tried to rob me again?"

Said dumbfuck whined, "Come on, Rory. I thought it was Hanna working tonight."

"Even worse."

Billy rose, as the clerk seemed to have the situation under control. "Um, I'm kind of in a hurry."

The clerk never even looked at him. "Don't worry about the gas. Just go, and if anyone asks, this never happened." The clerk put a foot on the robber's chest and pushed down until he whimpered.

A proper cop would have stayed and helped secure the scene, but Ulric thought Brandy might be in danger. Speaking of Ulric. The phone he'd dropped had hung up. Billy dialed as he jumped into his car and peeled out of the station.

"What the fuck happened?" Ulric yelled.

"Robbery. I'm on my way to Brandy now."

"Good. Because turns out she might have been the target all along."

"Explain. Quickly."

"While there's not much being released to the public about the prison massacre, Dorian managed to hijack the group that's discussing the case." Since the pandemic, many processes moved online. It created new ways to acquire information. "One of the cops on the scene said the killer, or killers—which seems more likely—left a message. Gruff must die."

"I don't see how that indicates Brandy is the target. Sounds more like a personal vendetta against me." Probably some scumbag pissed Billy caught his ass.

"I'm not done. That wasn't the only thing drawn. A heart with the initials BL + CJ."

"And?" The initials might only be a coincidence.

"Because I wasn't done." Ulric kept talking. "One of the surviving prison guards who'd been on vacation when this all went down said it referred to Clive Johnson and an old flame of his."

"I assume it's the same Clive Johnson I busted for a heist that resulted in a few people dead." He noted the lights of a vehicle coming from the opposite direction.

"One and the same. Turns out Clive has a history with Brandy. They dated for a bit and broke up right about the time you arrested him. Despite going to jail, he didn't take it well. She changed her phone number and went unlisted. The fucker remained obsessed. He wrote hundreds of letters to her. The content was so crazy they just threw them out."

"Why wouldn't she have told me about her crazy criminal ex?" Billy grumbled.

"Most likely because it's been years and he was supposed to still be in jail."

He peeled into the motel parking lot, noting the light was off in the office. He kept talking to Ulric. "If Clive is still obsessed, he would want me out of the way. I can even see why he'd arrange to kidnap Brandy. But that doesn't explain how he's got all kinds of convicts working for him."

"My theory is he's some kind of cult leader. Convinced a bunch of convicts to join him on a murder spree and escaped."

"And Brandy is the first person he'd most likely look for." He slammed into the spot beside her car in the parking lot. "I'm at the motel." And to his relief, no other vehicles were parked. "I'll call you back once I check on Brandy."

He exited his car, his ears attuned for anything. He paused at the door to their rented room. He could smell it already. Someone had been here. Three people by his count, one reeking of cigarettes like the person who checked them in.

He slammed the key into the lock and flung open

the door. Only she was gone.

Someone had taken her. Exiting the room, he took deep breaths. Which direction? Her scent ended on the pavement, indicating she'd been moved by vehicle. His mind jumped to the car he'd passed coming back from the gas station. Had to be.

He slammed into his vehicle and called Ulric as he peeled onto the pavement in pursuit.

The moment Ulric answered, he blurted out, "Brandy's gone." It hurt to say through his tight jaw.

"Oh fuck."

"I think I might have seen the car that took her." He sped, not caring if the road advised seventy kilometers an hour. He pushed it. His SUV could handle it.

"Don't kill yourself," Ulric admonished. "You're not good to Brandy dead."

He didn't slow down. The dark and his speed almost made him miss the car parked in the woods. His headlights briefly illuminated the taillights as he passed. He slammed on his brakes and reversed.

"I might have found the car," he huffed to Ulric. "I'm sending you my location." He thumbed his phone to drop a map pin in a text to Ulric.

"Maybe you should wait for backup."

"No time. I'm going for a look." He hung up as he exited his vehicle to investigate. No one sat in the car, but he didn't need to open the door to smell Brandy.

She was here. In the woods. In danger.

That was enough to bring forth his beast.

18

Brandy woke in a cave of all places. Damp, smelly, and mostly dark, given the only source of light was a lantern sitting on the ground. Its feeble glow didn't allow her to see the ceiling or much of the floor for that matter. Probably a good thing because the rank smell didn't inspire confidence.

How had she gotten here?

Last thing she remembered was opening the motel room door expecting Billy. Instead she found the clerk from the motel office and two rather large men, who proceeded to shove a smelly rag into her face.

Roofied again. Not good. Billy would be losing his mind. If Billy was okay. Had they gotten to him first?

She rose and noticed she had been laid on a bed of clothing. Literally shirts, pants, even jackets, piled atop slime.

Wait, that was poop. Bat poop. The moment she

thought it, a rustling overhead had her hugging her upper body. Why all the bats in her life lately?

"At last, you're awake, my love."

It couldn't be. That voice. That wording... The deepest of chills gripped her. "Clive?" Said really hoping she'd misheard. It had been so long.

"It's me, my love." He stepped into the light, changed and yet recognizable. Her crazy ex-boyfriend, his skin puffy and flushed, lips a brilliant red, eyes pure black. His hair hung limp and greasy.

The shock almost dropped Brandy on her ass as she managed a faint, "I thought you were in jail." Behind bars where he belonged. It had been years since she'd even thought about that brief moment of insanity. Shouldn't he be over his obsession by now?

"Ah yes, my prison. A miserable punishment made doubly so because I knew you must have been so distraught at our separation. Curse the bastards conspiring to keep us apart."

Ten years and he still believed they were together. She'd really dodged a bullet when she broke up with Clive. He'd hidden the crazy for a while. Once she recognized it, though, she took steps. He didn't have a chance to hurt her, and yet she'd never been happier than when he'd been put behind bars for life. The armed robbery got him in custody, and then they were able to tie him to the murder of some women. That put him away for a very long time, and she'd gone on with her life.

Apparently, he'd not done the same.

Rather than address his insanity, she asked, "Where are we?"

"My palace." He swept a hand. "Isn't it grand?"

"It's a bat-shit-filled cave."

"Is this how you thank me for providing you a home?" His timbre dropped ominously.

Brandy didn't cower. Appeasing him wouldn't be enough. Clive was a psycho killer. "A home has things like furniture, running hot water, a kitchen, some windows to let in some sunshine."

"Ingrate."

"I know. It's horrible of me, which is why I am going to leave."

"Don't be cross at me, my love. I am sure, whatever the issue, we can work through it. No need for you to leave. Not after all we've suffered. Now that we've reunited, we can be together." He dropped his voice an octave to add, "Forever." It might have been spookier if he'd not added a villainous muah-ha-ha on the end.

It made everything next-level ridiculous. "For Pete's sake, Clive. How many times do I have to say we're over?" She'd thought once he hit jail that would be end of it. Nope. He kept calling. So she changed her number, and the harassment stopped. She never assumed he'd still be obsessed this many years later.

"As if I would have listened. You and I are meant to be."

"No we're not. I've moved on. I'm with someone else now."

"Gruff." He practically hissed the word.

She froze. "How do you know about Billy?"

"Because I've been watching. It took me forever to find you, and then I had to be careful lest they try and keep us apart. Didn't you get my messages?"

"What messages?" she asked through stiff lips, even as it hit her. Those emails she'd been getting, those texts, they must have been Clive. Finding out he'd been watching and sending threatening messages, plotting this entire time, made Brandy feel quite sick. "How did you get out of jail early?" Had she missed a chance to remind them at his parole hearing that he wasn't a nice guy?

"By the best of luck. You see, I spent a lot of time in solitary. Bastards kept saying I was a danger to others. It was there I discovered his existence."

"Who?"

"The night janitor. Only that was just a cover. He only came in at night, not only because of his allergy to sunlight but because it was the best time for him to feed. Every night a different prisoner in solitary. He visited me the most often since I refused to obey their stupid rules. At first, I was helpless when he fed on me. But over time, his power over me waned. I got used to the venom in his bite. On his last attempt, I only pretended to be under his spell. You should have seen his surprise when I turned the tables." Clive grinned, a grotesque parody. "That night I was the one who fed on him. Drank his dying last drop. And then I became what he used to be." He flashed his fangs. "Can you guess what I am?"

"Are you trying to say you're a vampire?" she asked skeptically. She'd always pictured them a lot more suave than this two-bit stalking criminal who'd lost any hotness he might have had.

"In the flesh. And now I have my queen. Together we will rule the night from our palace." He swept an arm as if this were a dream come true.

Someone save her from the vampire who was literally batshit crazy.

"I'm going to have to pass. But thanks for the offer." She began to walk in a direction, any direction, only to be stopped by his statement.

"You won't escape me and don't expect rescue either. If Gruff tries to come after me, he'll pay with his blood."

"Leave Billy out of this. He's done nothing to you."

"Hasn't he? That fucking pig put me behind bars and then stole my girl," Clive spat.

"He didn't steal anything. We broke up. You were in jail. I moved on. And look at you, now a free man. You can have any woman you want." Even as she'd advise any woman to run fast and far away.

"I want you."

A chilling reply. Before she could retort, a distant howl prickled her senses. A wolf. Could it be *her* wolf? She had to stall for time. "How did you find me?"

"With great difficulty. The first few minions who set forth from the prison with instructions didn't do as told. Distance makes them harder to control."

"Minions? What are you, like some evil supervillain? When are you growing a mustache?"

"Do not mock me." He took a step closer.

She took one back. "Then don't sound like a crazy person. How many people have you conned into helping you?" How many would she have to evade in order to escape?

"Too many to count anymore. I wasn't very good at it in the beginning. But once I was able to properly feed and glut myself, it became much easier." *Now I can just slip into their minds and take them.*

The whisper hit her hard because it came from inside her head!

Her eyes widened. "Stay out of my thoughts."

"No." He didn't even hesitate. *I did not wait for you all those years to have you play hard to get.*

He wasn't even touching her, and yet her skin crawled. "You still haven't said how you found me."

"By accident. Given I wanted vengeance on Gruff, I sent my minions to seek him out. You happened to be in some of the images they took during their surveillance."

The spying disturbed, especially since she and Billy had only been in public together a few times. But there was a bigger problem. "Your emails started before I met Billy."

"That's because my lawyer found the email address you were using to receive case updates. I knew you cared."

She wanted to throw up. The email had been set up anonymously and then forwarded to her main account. She'd done everything to separate herself from Clive. And he'd still found her.

"You sent your goons to kidnap me," she accused.

"Actually, my minions had planned to take Gruff, so imagine the surprise when he was followed to a wedding and his date happened to be you. The plan changed at that point."

"And these thugs had no problem with your orders?"

"Hardly ordering. They are my servants. They do as I command."

"Because you use your vampire mojo on them."

"They are happy to serve. I'll show you." He snapped his fingers. "Bring her to me."

From the shadows at his back, men—still wearing their bright jumpsuits from prison—shambled forth.

"You heard the boss," spat the bearded one. "He wants the girl."

And Brandy wanted away from this madness.

A new glow of light turned out to be someone entering the cave, holding another lantern aloft.

"Boss. I think we got—" was all the guy had a chance to say before being knocked down hard.

The wolf doing the knocking walked over him and entered the cave. Its white fur gleamed, but not as bright as its gaze, currently fixated on Clive.

"Kill the dog!" Clive pointed, and his minions shifted their attention.

"That's no dog," Brandy sassed. "Say hello to my boyfriend, Billy. Did I forget to mention he's a werewolf?"

19

BACK AT THE ABANDONED CAR, Billy couldn't control his abrupt shift, just like he couldn't leash his wolf once it broke free. His four paws no sooner hit the ground than he was running with only one imperative: find Brandy.

He bolted into the woods, following Brandy's scent, knowing he wasn't far behind. What he didn't count on?

Being attacked from above.

Someone landed on his back, a human by scent and shape, and yet different. It tried to use its flat-edged teeth to bite. His fur protected him from the pathetic attempt. Billy bucked the person off, and then he pounced, making sure to show the correct way to kill with a chomp.

The next person revealed themselves by hiding their corpulent shape behind a tree that didn't quite cover. They had a gun, which might have been tricky if they knew how to shoot. By the time they managed to squeeze off three clumsy shots, Billy was on them.

One more down.

He couldn't tell how many to go because the pair he'd just handled weren't the ones he'd been following. Worse, they distracted him from his mission.

Save Brandy.

He had to backtrack to locate her scent. Ended up attacked again on the way by none other than the office clerk herself. He'd been so dumb. They should have never stopped. At the same time, he couldn't have predicted how far this Clive's influence would reach.

What he didn't understand? The rabid desire by these people to help Clive. The guy he recalled didn't have a charismatic bone in his body and skated by on his looks.

When a bullet singed across Billy ribs, he howled before bloodying his fur as he ripped out a throat. The bloodlust took him and fueled his annoyance at these pests in his path. Rather than wait for them to attack, he changed tactics and went after them, quickly stalking and taking them out of the equation. Only one escaped. Billy let him go on purpose and followed, keeping him in sight as he threaded the forest to the bottom of a mountain. The man climbed the rocky escarpment, paused on a ledge, lighting a lantern left there before disappearing inside the mountain.

Billy bounded up stone and dirt, moving rapidly

for the horizontal crevice that stood at least ten feet tall and half as wide. As he passed into the mountain, so many scents assailed him. Bat droppings. Mice. Other creatures. Even a bear. But over top of it all, blood, death, and something unknown. Something other...

His wolf balked at the scent, but Billy pushed forward. Brandy had passed through recently.

A faint murmur indicated voices ahead, one of them most definitely feminine.

The passageway widened, and ahead of him, he could see the person who'd entered before him, standing as if in a doorway, speaking to someone. "Boss..."

Billy tuned him out the moment he glanced past into the cavern itself and saw Brandy. She stood, seemingly unharmed, looking beautifully defiant.

He leaped and slammed into the man in his path, knocking him and his light to the floor. The cavern was illuminated enough for him to take in the odd tableau. The guy wearing a tattered cloak around his shoulders. A man who had to be Clive but looking haggard.

"Kill the dog!" Clive pointed, and his minions shifted their attention.

"That's no dog," Brandy sassed. "Say hello to my boyfriend, Billy. Did I forget to mention he's a werewolf?"

"I don't fucking care. What are you waiting for? Take him out." Clive pointed at Billy.

Three thugs advanced. He actually recognized two

of them as brothers who'd been involved in a string of violent home invasions that left female residents either traumatized or dead.

He felt nothing at all as he attacked, going in low to take out the legs on one before twisting and lunging for the other, biting into a thigh and waiting for a crack before letting go.

Clive roared in rage. "Fucking losers. Do something!"

The third thug instead ran screaming, hands on his ears. "I am not listening. La-la-la-la."

Billy had no time to discern what the hell that was about.

Brandy, a smirk on her lips, head held high and in strong spirits, said, "My werewolf boyfriend is about to kick your ass."

Boyfriend?

Clive stared at him, looking slightly amused. "Well, I'll be damned, a werewolf. Unexpected and not, I guess. After all, look at me, a bona fide vampire."

Vampire? Well, that explained the smell.

Clive glowered as if he'd heard. If Billy had a human mouth, he would have said something along the line of, *Your ass is grass.*

To Billy's shock, he got a reply.

We haven't even started yet, dog. The voice inside his head had him shaking it wildly as if he could shake it free.

"Billy?" He could hear Brandy.

He could also hear the insidious whisper. *Run and leap from this mountain. Fly.*

Billy fought the compulsion.

Feel like chewing off your own paws?

He would taste undoubtedly yummy, but he held firm.

Rather than wait to see if the mental attacks would work, Billy ran for the fucker, four legs pumping, ready to rip out Clive's throat. As he got close enough to see the amusement in Clive's dark gaze, the voice shouted, *Stop.*

Billy stumbled and landed nose first. He quickly recovered and threw himself at Clive's legs, knocking him over.

The voice in his head yelled, *Do not fight.*

As if.

He snapped at Clive, narrowly missing the hands flailing to keep him from soft and vulnerable spots. He suddenly managed to sink his teeth into a hand, and Clive squealed.

That's not supposed to happen.

Billy regretted it, too, given the blood tasted like shit.

"You shouldn't have done that," grunted Clive, his body suddenly burning hot and quivering.

When it began shifting underneath, Billy threw himself to the side. Clive went from puffy-faced vampire to hideous bat.

The creature turned on him, its eyes no longer dark

orbs but red fiery pits. It hissed and lunged, fast and accurate, as if it knew which way he'd dive. The Clive-bat hit Billy hard and sent them to the ground, where they slid in the slimy bat shit. Gross.

He shook off the bat and rose to four feet, snarling. He'd barely had time to brace when Clive-bat was on him, slashing with claws, trying to bite with those teeth. A stripe down his back burned and brought a yelp to his muzzle.

Brandy screamed, "Leave him alone."

Why didn't she run?

Billy might have started the fight confidant, but that was when he thought he dealt with a man. Against a vampire who kept reading his mind, predicting his moves...

The next razor-sharp swipe burned with more intense cold. Billy hit the ground, sides heaving, as Clive knelt by him.

The vampire bat hissed, showing off canines that Billy didn't doubt would suck him dry.

His eyes widened as the sharp end of a stick punched through Clive's chest.

The bat gasped, keened, and then fell away from Billy, barely managing to crawl a few paces before collapsing.

Brandy was suddenly on her knees by Billy's side, cradling his head in her lap. "Billy! Speak to me."

He cocked open an eye and managed a very unwolf-like, "Woof."

"Baby." She hugged him tight. "I was so scared for you. I would have been really bummed to see the man I love die before my very eyes."

The man she loved.

The shock of it had him shifting, and bless Brandy's heart, she looked more fascinated than horrified as he pulled the switch.

"Baby," was the first thing he said.

"Oh, Billy." She sighed his name. Leaned down as if to kiss him when they heard it.

A rustle of sound. By the time he managed to crane to look behind her, the Clive-bat was escaping.

"We can't let him escape." Forget his wounds, Billy bolted to his feet and ran after Clive, not knowing what he'd do once he caught up. Two fists and a hanging dick weren't exactly deadly weapons against something sporting fangs and sharp teeth. Just ask his smarting back with its burning stripes.

As he reached the crevice entrance, he was just in time to see Clive-bat leap into the air and flap his wings while sending one last mental message.

I'll be back.

It was almost shocking that the words didn't come in a Schwarzenegger accent.

Brandy emerged from the cave at a run, yelling, "Something pissed off the bats!"

Indeed, he could hear the flutter of their leathery wings. He had just enough time to slam her to the side of the crevice before the bats emerged, a cloud of them frantically flapping in all directions before forming a cohesive swarm.

They enveloped Clive-bat, getting tangled in his wings, a cloud of tiny bodies that overwhelmed. Clive dropped, his wings flapping, shouting in his head, *Save me!*

The pressure in Billy's mind eased the moment Clive hit the apex of a dead tree, impaled upon the wood.

"Do you think he's dead this time?" Brandy asked, chewing her lower lip.

"I don't know. But I say we wait here for a bit just in case." Better the enemy they could see coming than the one readying an ambush.

"You need clothes and bandages." Before he could stop Brandy, she rushed back into the cave and emerged with a pile of castoffs from the top of the pile she'd been lying on—and the least bat-shit covered.

Despite his assertion he'd be fine, she insisted on checking his scratches, fretting over the fact she couldn't clean them properly. "What if those bats had rabies?" she exclaimed.

"The worst that will happen is a short-lived infection." Because his Lycan genes rendered him tough.

They sat side by side on the ledge and kept watch on Clive's body as night turned into dawn. The sun's early rays caused a chemical process in the giant Clive-bat that grossed out and fascinated all at once.

"He's melting." Brandy did a proper imitation of

the witch in *The Wizard of Oz*. A woman who, despite everything that happened, retained her good sense of humor.

He blurted out, "I love you."

Her smartass reply? "I know."

EPILOGUE

The country cousins came to the rescue not long after dawn. Apparently, Ulric contacted them for help since they were closest.

The cousins—no actual blood relation to Billy, unless the Lycan thing counted—took care of the bodies and the many abandoned cars spread out along the roads lining this part of the forest. They planned to make it all disappear.

Billy carried a protesting Brandy back to his SUV and drove to them to the motel where they could properly shower and ensure all their things were packed away.

When it came time to leave, one of the cousins volunteered to take Brandy's rental back to the city so they could share one vehicle.

It proved to be a dangerous choice. Brandy gave

him head while he drove, with one admonishment. "Don't crash."

He ended up pulling over and showing her why he loved his oversized SUV when he put down the seats in the back. She stripped the moment she realized he'd made them a bed. He joined her, kissing her like he hadn't made love to her twice already in the shower. This time was purely for pleasure and not relief they'd both survived.

He slid into her and grunted at the exquisite tightness of her. The perfection. Her hips rocked under him. Her soft pants spurred him on. Together they peaked, her orgasm gloriously loud.

While the pleasure rode him, he bit her in the same spot as before, only this time he did it quite intentionally and murmured, "My mate."

And he couldn't be happier. Because Brandy had taught him that by being alone and miserable, his parents had been winning. Only by allowing himself to be happy could he break the cycle of violence and misery.

Which was why when they got back to town he started seeing a therapist, and when he felt ready, he presented Brandy with a key to his place and said simply, "I love you. Move in with me."

Brandy snorted. "Dude, I haven't been home in ten days. There are tampons in your bathroom."

"So that's a yes?" he grumbled.

She smiled. "You couldn't get rid of me if you tried."

Good, because he had his eyes on a ring and hoped by this time next year to be calling her wife.

Ulric's new kitten explored his head of hair, a source of fascination for the little bugger. Blame Brandy. When she returned and demanded the return of her cat, he'd found himself missing the feline. Hence the sudden adoption.

It wasn't a replacement for love, but it would help fill that lonely hole while Ulric kept looking for Mrs. Right. And he'd been trying. Dated all kinds of women looking for *the one*.

Alas, the only female pussy interested in him weighed only a few pounds and had chosen to go sniffing in his beard and gotten caught. Like seriously tangled. Paws, claws, poor kitty appeared quite caught. Not that she panicked.

The kitten went to sleep.

Ulric went bolting for help.

Given he didn't want to deal with the amusement of his pack brothers, or hurt his little princess trying to extricate her, he chose to visit the vet down the block, open until eight on Thursdays, which was lucky for him.

Less ideal?

The absolutely gorgeous woman who took one look at him and laughed.

Ulric wasn't in the mood for levity because staring at Dr. Iris, it hit him like a lightning bolt.

I've found her. The one.

And just his luck, she wore a wedding ring.

GET READY FOR THE NEXT FURRY ADVENTURE IN HONEY'S WEREWOLF.

For more books and fun see EveLanglais.com

www.ingramcontent.com/pod-product-compliance
Lightning Source LLC
LaVergne TN
LVHW031539060526
838200LV00056B/4573